I0826196

27 Flagship Cove

Yolanda M. Johnson

Literary Wonders! Media Group

Literary Wonders! Media Group

Greensboro, North Carolina

©2013 by
Yolanda M. Johnson

All rights reserved. No part of this book may be reproduced in any form without permission in writing from the publisher, except in the case of brief quotations embodied in critical articles and reviews. For more information or questions, please address the author or contact LW Media Group, PO BOX 13727, Greensboro, NC 27405.

This book is a work of fiction. Names, characters, places and incidents are products of the author's imagination or are used fictitiously. However, some instances and events are true and names have been changed to protect the innocent *and* the guilty.

ISBN 10:0-9770403-2-1
ISBN 13:978-0-9770403-2-2
Library of Congress Control Number: 2013906561

Printed in the United States of America

Also by
Yolanda M. Johnson

My Daughter's Keeper
Circumstances
Revelations

Anthologies
Crimes of Passion: The Anthology
She Has a Big 'But'!: Get Past Your Excuses & Realize Your Dreams

For Delina, Kemet and Remii

Praises for ***Circumstances.***

"***Circumstances*** is an engaging tale of a daughter's quest to find inner peace while dealing with a dysfunctional relationship with her mother. Yolanda M. Johnson touches on issues that may shock you; however you won't be able to pull yourself away from the pages." --*Shelia M. Goss , Essence Magazine's Best Selling Author of My Invisible Husband and Dallas Morning News Best Selling Author of Roses Are Thorns, Violets are True*

"***Circumstances*** draws the reader in from the intriguing introduction. It is a passionate story that teleports the reader into the minds and lives of the characters. The dialog is conversational and as you read, you hear the perspectives of the characters, their conflict, and their anguish. I believe author Yolanda Johnson has written an empathetically real and unique story that is as easy to love as it is to read."--*Bennie Patridge III "The MANual*

"Yolanda Johnson is a powerful new voice in the literary world. ***Circumstances*** leaves you wanting more!" --*Sylvia Willis Lett - I Wish I Had Waited" Dallas Morning News #1 Best seller*

"From the opening page to the dramatic ending, ***CIRCUMSTANCES*** is a powerful tale of love and forgiveness. Johnson pulls no punches as she vividly describes the mental, emotional and physical impact of abuse and not just to the victim." –*Monique Bruner Delta Reviewer" Real Page Turners*

Praises for ***Revelations***

Even though it was recommended reading ***Circumstances*** first, I did the opposite but ***Revelations*** definitely stood on its own. Yolanda draws you in as if you're actually there. Whenever I tried to pause, I found myself turning the page. The ending was definitely shocking! Didn't see that coming. This is a must read and I can't wait to read ***Circumstances***. Thank you Yolanda! ~~*The Facial Lady*

Yolanda M. Johnson writes another powerful story with ***Revelations***, the follow up to ***Circumstances***. After the shocking ending in ***Circumstances***, it was hard to imagine what other surprises were in store, but Ms. Johnson doesn't disappoint. More secrets are revealed, and there is nothing predictable about the twists and turns in this tale. ~~*Melissa Bennett, Carbon Copy Editing*

You'll have to read the book to see if you would be able to endure ten minutes in Renee's shoes before looking for the fastest car leaving town. ***Revelations*** is a roller coaster ride that takes you on a journey of love, hate, inner-strength, forgiveness, and a true test of patience. ~~*T. Price*

Revelations by Yolanda Johnson delves into the dynamic and somewhat tumultuous relationship between a mother and daughter. It deals with love, heartbreak and family scandals. This emotional read will have readers talking about ***REVELATIONS*** long after they've read the last page. Kudos Ms. Johnson for delivering another dramatic page turner. ~~*Shelia M. Goss, Emma Award Finalist and author of Delilah and Ruthless*

A Note from the Author

I've said it often when asked, *Yolanda, what genre do you write?* And, my answer is always, *I don't like to categorize my writing. I don't like being put in a box. If I absolutely had to generalize my writing, I would say that I mostly write about women's issues. I've written and will continue to write about issues that women face in my fiction and non-fiction works, whether they be health issues, relationship issues, mental issues, personal or professional issues.*

And, this is one of the reasons I ventured into mystery crime thrillers. While others are watching the plethora of reality shows, I'm watching CSI and NCIS. My favorite by far is NCIS. I love Gibbs, played by Mark Harmon. Many of you'd be surprised to know that before I made the decision to major in technology, I considered majoring in forensics. I'm so glad I didn't because my stomach has always been on the queasy side. However, I've always been fascinated with cracking crimes.

I've also been asked the question, *"Why do you call it a Christian Thriller?"* Well the answer is simply, *"Because everyone in the church isn't a saint and every saint in the church has gone through trials and that includes criminal ones."*

It is my hopes that you enjoy this first installment and introduction to the Tommie Lane Christian Thriller Series, as well as future installments. Thanks to you all, for indulging in my writing adventures.

God Bless!

Yolanda M. Johnson

Acknowledgements

For anything that I do, I am required, and feel the urge to thank God. Nothing I do, that does not include Him will, simply, fail.

I will also, always, thank my husband, Gregory Bryant. If you all knew what he had to put up with or the abundance of support he provides me as I live my dream, you'd be surprised. He is my sounding board and my stress reliever. He is my provider and my reality checker. I love you and thank you for who you are.

I'd like to thank those who give me great writing material. I'm grateful for my past experiences because they make even better writing material.

And, thank you to readers of my material. I am thankful that you choose my stories to entertain you and I am grateful for your reviews—both good and bad.

Limon, CO
Wednesday, October 5, 2011

Lucien Guillory looked one last time in the mirror. Today was the day he would be leaving the place he'd called home for fifteen years.

His lady, Paige, had made sure he looked good as he left confinement and smelled freedom. She had bought him a black suit, a white shirt, a dark tie and pair of size thirteen dress shoes.

In the presence of prison guards, Lucien had shaved his face clean and cut off his ten-inch dreadlocks. His salt-and-peppered hair was now short and neat. He couldn't remember the last time he'd worn a suit or looked this good outside prison garb.

Still got it, he thought to himself. Lucien stood five-foot-eight, and although he was considered short in most superficial circumstances, he carried his height well. And, at one-hundred-sixty-five pounds, he was thin, but all muscle. His light brown skin and coy smile always assured he'd have no problem with the ladies.

Normally, Lucien would have gone home—to Atlanta, Georgia. It was where his parents were from, where he was raised. His father was a police officer, his mother disabled and retired. Legend had it that she practiced witchcraft. And, although Lucien was close to his mother, he and his father hadn't seen eye to eye.

Lucien could remember the last time he had seen his father. Shortly after he was incarcerated, Mr. Guillory paid Lucien a visit—to tell him not to expect any future visits and to plan on never seeing him again. As a matter of fact, Lucien can remember his father's last words to him, *"You're dead to me, and leave your mother be."* Yes, those were the last words Lucien heard his father spew before he walked away, never to be seen again.

As if he wasn't already bitter, watching his father walk away, Lucien promised to himself that one day he would seek revenge on his father. Unfortunately, Lucien would never get the chance to carry out his plan—his father was killed two years later in a gang initiation gone wrong. The gang inductee had no idea he was robbing a police officer's home and he had no idea that Mr. Guillory was at home.

Mr. Guillory had surprised the robber—he got off one shot and so did the robber. In an odd turn of events, the two gun-toting black men canceled each other out. When news reached the Colorado Department of Corrections in Limon, Lucien wasn't the least bit phased. Poetic Justice is what he called it.

Now, as Lucien stood in the mirror, he thought about what he'd do once he smelled freedom. He swore he'd get a double-bacon cheeseburger, with a side of onion rings and a chocolate milkshake from Burger King—his favorite.

He had been used to the cold Colorado winters, and although the calendar said October he knew it wasn't unusual for snow to cover the ground this time of year. He was looking forward to it. He would make snow angels, and then he and Paige would stay held up for days while he re-familiarized himself with the female anatomy. The next thing he'd do . . . make sure he'd seek revenge on the people who helped to prosecute him. To him that included everyone from the judge to the jury *and* those who testified against him. This time, he'd be more careful. This time, he would make sure he didn't get caught.

Yes, today, he'd finally be released. After much research, numerous appeals, and countless letters to governor Hickenlooper, he would finally be a free man. He had spent several years in this prison cell—accused of stabbing a woman twenty-two times in his car. He didn't deny his crime, but he had made sure the American Judicial System followed its own rules. No one said it was fair, but it *was* the law, and . . . the American way.

Several things worked in Lucien's favor—the arresting officer failed to read him his Miranda rights, and the fine men of the Denver Police Department had beat a confessions out of him. They had beaten him for nearly forty-five minutes, and tried to cover it up. False statements were given, and people were bought off in an effort to make sure that Lucien went to, and *stayed* in prison.

In addition, the arresting officer testified that that two people had observed Lucien and a female friend fighting in a car while parked at a neighborhood park. When the police arrived, the officer stated that the inside of Lucien's car was covered with blood. The woman was on the floor of the car and appeared to have several stab wounds. She was announced DOA. Lucien had testified that he did not deliberately kill the young woman, that under the influence of alcohol, he had blacked out.

The officer officially testified that he read Lucien his Miranda rights. During cross examination, the officer stated he did not remember if he had read Lucien his Miranda rights or not and that he only saw blood on Lucien's clothing—not in the car as he had originally testified.

Even so, Lucien was a black man in the state of Colorado and he had been accused of viciously killing a white woman. He was charged with first-degree murder and sentenced to death by injection.

In his appeal requests, Lucien argued that his trial should have ended in a mistrial or dismissed, because his right to due process and a fair and impartial jury were violated. His lawyer had produced evidence that Lucien was possibly set up. It was said that Lucien was having an affair with the arresting officer's wife. If that didn't add fuel to the fire, one of the jurors happened to the brother-in-law of the arresting officer's wife and failed to disclose the information until deliberations. During which time, several jurors sent out notes to the court regarding their concern that one juror was biased.

Another juror had previously pled guilty to assault, domestic violence and drug and alcohol charges—information that was omitted from his pre-selection questionnaire.

With all this working for him, a new attorney and fifteen years of good behavior, Lucien was happy he'd escaped death and he'd never see another day inside his jail cell.

It's true when they say what's done in the dark will come to the light. Perhaps the real reason Lucien was released, fourteen years later, after confessing to his wife one evening—after too much alcohol—one of the officers who had helped beat Lucien within an inch of his life and falsified the police report, came forward with some damaging information. A confession and recorded video caught all forty-five minutes of the beating—forty-five minutes and thirty-six seconds to be exact. A federal probe ensued and other damaging evidence was found from various sources, including Lucien's crooked attorney.

And now, he could thank those very same people for making this day possible for him. He would have to seek out the officer that got him off and thank him . . . then, he'd kill him. In fact, he'd seek them all out, torture and then kill them.

Lucien slicked his mustache one last time and smiled at himself in the mirror. He looked around the six-by-eight cell, its hard bed and toilet that could easily touched from that bed, and what had been his belongings for the last fifteen years. A small photo of his mother was taped to one of the walls, and on the only shelf in his cell were tons of law books and a bible. He grabbed the photo from the wall, tucked in between the pages of the bible and tucked the bible under his arm. Spending time between Canon City and Limon, death row left much to be desired. No, he would not miss this place at all.

"Let's go Guillory," a heavily armed security guard with a deep voice said. Lucien stopped and turned to look at the cage he'd called home for so long. “If I ever see you again, it will be too soon,” he told the guard.

“Just remember, three strikes and you’re out. You’ll be back.” With that, three security guards escorted him from the prison.

Two

Lucien looked up to the sky once he stood outside the gates of the Colorado Corrections Facility. He closed his eyes, smiled and let the warm sunlight shine upon his clean-shaven face. Piles of snow and clear streets were signs of a recent snow storm. The sun glistening off the white snow enhanced the shine of everything around it, brightening the chilly Wednesday afternoon. Lucien had a sudden appreciation for things he had previously taken for granted—snow, sunlight and plain old clean, crisp air.

He had always said if he ever made it out of this hellhole, he'd kiss the ground once outside the prison. Now that that day had come, he thought against it. The snow had turned the dirt into a muddy oasis. After all, he couldn't wrinkle or dirty his tailored suit, and he certainly didn't want Paige to see him kissing a dirty ground—she might think he was weak and he couldn't have any of that.

After the prison gates closed, Lucien turned around and looked one last time at the prison. Its illumination much brighter than the day he arrived. "Goodbye and go straight to hell!" he yelled to the unknowing structure. Even though he wasn't Catholic, he crossed his chest, gave a Hail Mary, and headed towards Paige's Tahoe.

As though he had expected it, and on cue, Paige ran into Lucien's arms. "Baby!" she shouted. "I've missed you so much. I'm so glad you're finally out of that place."

The two held each other in a strong embrace and kissed as if it was the last time they'd see each other.

After a couple of minutes, Lucien stood back to take her in. Even though she wasn't the type he was normally into, Paige had always been attractive to Lucien. And today, she looked especially nice. Her sandy blonde hair was curled and parted on the side. He could tell that she had added platinum blonde highlights. Her pale skin had a tinge of tan color, and she wore make-up—not a lot, but just the amount Lucien liked.

Even though Paige looked great with no make-up, Lucien believed every woman could benefit from a little make-up, whether it was lipstick, blush or mascara. On this day, Paige wore fire engine red lipstick, black eye liner that formed a cat-eye and black mascara. Her red tailored pantsuit was accessorized with a cream lace sheath, pearl earrings and a pearl necklace—her patent black patent leather boots had four-inch heels.

One of the things Lucien loved about Paige was, even though she was what others might consider a tad bit over weight, she was naturally sexy with curves in all the right places and she didn't feel the need to dress trampy.

Sure Lucien had had his share of beautiful women, but Paige was different from the rest. Perhaps it was the fact that she was the only one that stood by him when he went to prison—and the only one that hadn't judged him. Or perhaps it was because she wasn't after financial gain, or simply because she accepted him for exactly who he was.

Lucien drew in a deep breath, looked at Paige one last time before getting into her SUV. Paige pointed the black Chevy Tahoe west on I-70 and drove away from the prison. Lucien looked into the passenger side mirror and watched as the structure got smaller and smaller—until it finally disappeared.

"Where are we headed?" Lucien asked her, unable to keep his eyes off her. He noted, once more, how well she looked and good she smelled. He smiled to himself.

"Your favorite place," she answered with a smile, not taking her eyes off the road.

"Your place?"

"No silly. Where was the first place you told you wanted to go as soon as you got out?" She took her eyes off the road or a moment to see if he could remember.

"I don't remember." Lucien squinted trying to remember what he had told her. There were so many things he wanted to do when he got out.

"You'll see," she said as if she knew what he was thinking.

After much catching up and twenty minutes later, Paige pulled into a Burger King drive-thru.

"Wow, do you know how long I have dreamed about a Triple Decker with bacon and hot Onion rings? " he looked at her amazed. "But I know you didn't dress like that just to go to Burger King."

"Just go with the program man. You sure ask a lot of questions." They both laughed.

After receiving their order, Paige pulled into an empty parking space and they enjoyed their meal and afterwards completed it with a chocolate milkshake. Lucien was enjoying himself and his newfound freedom, but he couldn't help but think about his plan. He would put it into place soon, but for now, he tried to concentrate on Paige and his second chance—or was it his third? He knew he'd have to get it right this time, or there'd be *no* more chances.

Three

Paige pulled up to the gate of her Englewood condo complex. It was actually an investment property she had recently purchased and furnished. She felt more comfortable bring Lucien here than her home in Aurora. After all, she didn't completely trust Lucien. Her letters to him while he was in prison were always postmarked with a post office box.

Lucien had been her best friend's stepfather before he had gone to jail. She could never figure out her attraction to him—why she, an educated, middle class white woman, would be involved with someone who had been accused of a murder and on his way to prison. And, she couldn't figure out why she had chosen to stoop so low as to become intimate with someone she looked up to as a father-figure.

Lucien had told her that she did have a choice— she could commit to him or she could walk away, no questions asked. Even she was surprised when she told him that she'd stay by his side, no matter how much time he'd spend in prison. Even so, part of her knew that had she walked away from him, she would be one of those he had vowed to seek revenge against.

She made sure that while Lucien was in prison, she didn't outwardly date anyone. She kept any secret rendezvous as discreet as possible because she knew Lucien had eyes on the outside, and that he was receiving updates on a regular basis. So, to pass the time away, she gave everything to her career.

"Nice place," Lucien finally spoke. "They look brand new." Paige had told Lucien she was staying in her father's home until its recent sale. From what he could remember, the old family home left much to be desired.

"They're about six months old. I got in at a good deal."

Lucien thought about what she said. He knew that Paige did well for herself, but he wasn't sure how well. He knew she knew that she worked IT for a Fortune 500 Company. He scanned his memory trying to remember all the things he knew about her. He knew she was from a middle class family—Irish and Indian to be exact—and had lived in Colorado all her life. He knew that her father had died some time ago and that she was estranged from her mother. When Lucien had asked about her mother, Paige always said she didn't want to talk about it and changed the subject.

He scanned the new development under construction, and ventured to say the condos before him had to be going for at least half a million dollars. He knew there was no way the sale of the old family home could have yielded enough profit to purchase her new home. Yes, he knew that Paige would serve well in funding his crime spree.

The pair exited the car and headed up to Paige's condo. The elevator let them out on the twelfth floor. When she opened the door, Lucien could see how spacious the condo was from the hallway. Looking straight back, he could see a breathtaking view of a lake and a beautiful greenway.

Paige stood aside and allowed Lucien into her home. The foyer was large with a sofa table and large mirror on each side and a large crystal chandelier hung from the ceiling.

"How big is this place?" Lucien asked admiring the condo. He was sure his earlier estimate of half a million was inaccurate. This very well could have been a million dollar property.

"About thirty-seven hundred square feet," Paige answered him.

"Impressive," Lucien said. "Mind if I look around?"

"Not at all. I'll give you a tour." Paige showed Lucien every inch of the three bedroom, four bath condo before Lucien asked, "What's that smell?"

"That, sir, would be your dinner. I remembered you saying that your favorite meal was fillet mignon, lobster, garlic mashed potatoes and asparagus. "

"Don't tell me that's what's cooking."

"It's actually done, just warming right now." Paige stopped and chuckled to herself for a minute.

"What's so funny?" Lucien asked.

"Well, it took me a while to figure out that sweet tea was a southern thing." They both laughed.

Lucien was rarely impressed, but Paige had caught him off guard. Lucien was used to women using their bodies to get what they wanted from him and none of them could cook. And now, here he was, with this woman who had her own and knew how to cook a great piece of steak. She knew from the beginning that Lucien had nothing, or so he wanted her to believe that. Lucien made sure he told no one that after his father had died, his mother had split money from an insurance policy she secretly held for him. The policy was for 1.2 million dollars and Lucien had access to those funds the minute he stepped out of prison. But why spend his money, when he could spend someone else's? Besides, Paige was more than just money to him. She served as a temporary companion, his eyes and ears and accessory to his forthcoming crime spree.

Lucien walked over the kitchen island and watched Paige as she made Lucien a drink. He paid special attention to her appearance. Before, he was just happy to say he had a woman. Now that he observed her, he realized that she wasn't someone he would normally be attracted to.

Although he did like white women, he liked them thin, with blonde hair and light eyes. Paige had blonde hair, she stood about five-foot-seven and her overweight frame was somewhere around two-hundred-ten pounds. After all these years, this is the woman who had stood by him, made sure he had all the things he needed, money on his books and an occasional conjugal visit. The thought of it all, made him hot for her at this very moment.

He took hold of her waist and kissed her passionately.

"Have I thanked you lately?" he asked.

"You may have at one point or another. But you're very welcome," she answered.

The two kissed for a few more moments before Paige led him to the master bedroom. Lucien laid her on the king sized bed and showed her just how much he appreciated her. The two made love for what seemed like hours. Before they knew it, they had both drifted off into a deep sleep.

*****

Lucien opened his eyes and looked around the immaculate bedroom. He could get used to this, but knew it wasn't his reality. He had never been a one-woman man, and even if he used Paige as his main girl, she may never accept the fact that she wouldn't be his only girl. Besides, Lucien knew that once Paige helped him carry out his plot of revenge, she would have to become a casualty. That was just how it had to be.

He showered in the master bathroom and looked at himself in the mirror. He could hear Paige stirring about in the kitchen. Even though the love that they had just made was the best he could remember, he was already bored. He had to get his head straight and make sure he executed his plan properly. He ran a brief plan through his mind before he joined Paige who was putting the finishing touches on dinner. The dining table had been set, complete with dinner napkins, candles and wine.

"I sure hope you're hungry, "she said when she felt his presence.

"After the hurting you put on me, you better believe I am." Lucien's eyes widened when he spotted the bottle of wine on the table. "*Silver Oak Napa Valley Cabernet Sauvignon 2008*? I know you didn't buy this bottle of wine at Safeway. Where'd you get this from?"

"A winery. During one of our girl's weekends. We took a tour of one of the Napa Valley wineries."

"Well, this isn't exactly a cheap bottle of wine," Lucien said matter-of-factly.

"It didn't cost that much," Paige assured him.

"At least a hundred bucks," he said. Paige smiled.

The two dove into their dinner and Lucien savored every morsel. He couldn't remember the last time he had a meal so tasty.

The two ate and made small talk until a breaking news story caught their attention. A reporter from KUSA Channel 9 News reported that former convicted murderer Lucien Guillory had been released from prison after winning an appeal. Paige turned up the volume.

"You'll remember back in 1997, Mr. Guillory was convicted of killing Barbra Anne Harrison of Aurora, Colorado. Initial reports state that Mr. Guillory was caught in the act as he stabbed his victim more than twenty-six times at a park inside his car. The details were sketchy not to mention accounts of police corruption by the Denver Police Department. Many say that they are not surprised that Mr. Guillory's conviction was overturned. As for the victim's family, we have been unsuccessful in our attempts to reach anyone. The victim's only known relative, a daughter, was last said to be living in an Aurora suburb. We'll bring you more details on this breaking story as they become available."

Paige clicked off the television with the universal remote. "So what's the plan?" she asked Lucien.

"Just as we discussed. We'll lay low for a while. Then, when they least expect it, we'll make our move."

"All of them?"

"All of them," Lucien said as he stared out into space.

Four

Greensboro, NC
Monday, August 20, 2012

Tiffany Jordan looked at the time on her cell phone that lay on the nightstand next to her bed. The digital display read *4:27 a.m.* She had awakened for the third time since *2:00 a.m.* to urinate. She made a mental note to schedule an appointment with her doctor.

She got out of her king-sized bed and its warmth and exposed herself to the coldness of her ceiling fan. Everyone had his or her vice, and one of hers was sleeping under the ceiling fan, no matter what the temperature was outside, and escaping the chill under her electric blanket.

"Why you just not turn off fan?" her friend Kim Pham had asked. Tiffany replied that she didn't complain about any of her friend's strange habits so she should let hers be.

Tiffany turned on the light to the master bathroom, headed to the toilet, and popped a squat. Her frequent urination had gone on for about a week now and she was almost certain that she had a urinary tract or kidney infection. She also knew that the cause was possibly all the Diet Coke she drank and the lack of water she had consumed on a daily basis.

She washed her hands after she was done with her business, taking in the scent of the Fresh Bamboo hand soap she had purchased from Bath and Body Works, letting the hot water warm her hands before drying them with a paper towel. As she dried her hands, she noticed visible bags under her hazel eyes. She would make sure to apply ice cubes to them when she woke up.

She turned off the light and reclaimed her position in between her sixteen-hundred-threat-count sheets, electric blanket and duvet. Although she turned the ringer off both her home and cell phones at night, she noticed the display on her cell phone was lit. The alerts showed that she had three missed calls.

Who in the world would be calling me at this hour? she thought to herself.

She had had the number for only eight months and for the last three months, she'd been receiving calls from an unknown caller. At first, the calls started with her home phone and then carried over to her cell phone.

She tried to think back and wonder if perhaps she had signed up for anything that required her phone number. The calls could very well be coming from some sort of solicitor or telemarketer. She had been out shopping a few weeks ago and signed up for email alerts at her local Bath and Body Works and Trader Joe's. They *did* ask for her phone number, but disclaimed that they would not sell her information to any third-party company. Even so, certainly they wouldn't be calling at this god-awful hour.

She powered off her cell phone and tried to go back to sleep, but she got the eeriest feeling—as if someone was in her home, watching her. She heard odd noises and creaks.

The sounds very well could have been her new house making noises that most houses did when they settled into the soil. She had just purchased the house less than a year earlier and her builder had warned her that the house would make those very noises for a while.

She had purchased the house after receiving a hefty twenty-million dollar divorce settlement from her scoundrel of an ex-husband, Richard. They had divorced due to infidelity and irreconcilable differences. Tiffany had found out that Richard had many mistresses, but one was having his child.

She had known for a long while that he was cheating, but she waited patiently, gathering all the evidence she could. Her mother didn't raise no fool. She was always taught to think before she leaped and she was smart enough to know that you didn't just up and leave a fifteen year marriage empty handed.

After the judge was done dividing assets, Tiffany was awarded twenty-million dollars, half the proceeds from the sale of their home they shared in Dallas, investment property in San Diego and Aspen, the Jaguar, half of Richard's investments and half of a secret account he didn't think she knew about—the one he used to keep his mistress and unborn child in a home and dripping in diamonds.

By the time she was done with Richard, she had obtained half of everything he owned and Richard's 'baby momma' sued him for full custody of their child and ended up leaving him for another man. Funny thing that karma is.

Wanting to leave her past behind, Tiffany visited several states and cities at the requests of her girlfriends, all with the intent of making one of them her new home. She knew she didn't want to go back to Colorado—there were far too many memories, more bad than good.

Her friend Kim suggested she relocate to San Diego, while her friend Maria Santiago suggested she make Key West her new home. It took several months, but after much nudging, she decided to move to North Carolina where her best friend Tommie Lane lived. Tommie was a seasoned detective with the Greensboro police department.

Tiffany was also impressed by the change of seasons and the lovely fall coloring and foliage. It sure beat thirty below temps and numerous winter days with a foot or more of snow. Tommie assured her that it barely snowed in Greensboro . . . they had a snow storm right after Tiffany moved to the southern city. She wanted to get out of dodge, but Tommie convinced her to give it a shot . . . and she did.

She didn't know what she was trying to prove, buying the eighty-six hundred square foot, three-story home, but after she met with the builder, she knew it was the house for her. In addition to the large pool and hot tub out back, the immaculate home overlooked Lake Jeanette, a prestigious neighborhood in the southern city.

One would argue that five bedrooms and eight-and-a-half baths, was far too much for just one person. Tiffany begged to differ. In addition to her many excuses for purchasing the home, her girlfriends would always have a place to stay during their monthly girls weekend or anytime either of them wanted to visit or needed a place to stay. She thought it silly that they'd pay for a hotel when she had so much space.

A loud thud interrupted Tiffany's thoughts. She shot straight up in her bed and looked around the large bedroom. She got out of bed and removed her friend, *Ruger,* from its case, which was tucked away in the nightstand next to her bed.

Having a friend like Detective Tommie Lane meant she *had* to own a gun. Tommie insisted upon it, in fact she insisted *all* her friends were packing.

"Folks are crazier today than they ever were," Tommy would say. "And I want to make sure each of my girls has protection. Don't you hesitate to use it if you feel threatened. But some of you have a few screws loose. I don't know if I feel comfortable with *all* of you carrying a gun," Tommie said, referring to Jillian. Everyone thought there was something off about their friend, but they loved her so much, they accepted it.

"Just remember to make sure you use it only when you have to. And remember never point a gun at someone unless you plan on using it."

Tiffany made sure her gun was loaded and cocked as she exited her bedroom, rounded the catwalk and walked down the spiral staircase. Suddenly the thunder broke so loud, Tiffany thought something had crashed into her home. When she realized it was storming, she shook the notion that someone was in the house. She took one last look at the alarms system and after she was sure it was secured, she headed back up the staircase. She wasn't going to act like a prisoner in her own home.

Once she returned to her bedroom, Tiffany eyed the security alarm one last time and walked to the large bay window. She scanned the land below. Her bedroom was on the third floor and there was a landing deck below that opened off the kitchen and the family room. Down the stairs to the left was a nice floral garden with a bench. Down the stairs to the right was a large deck and two-story gazebo. Straight ahead was a large infinity pool and spa. She admired the lake, perhaps it was the deciding factor in buying this home.

She watched as the raindrops fell furiously, splashing into the dark murky mass. It wasn't until a bolt of lightning lit of the night sky that she decided to hide under the protection of her covers, and try once more to get some shuteye. She heard noises again, but when she concluded that it was the storm, she fluffed her pillow, assumed that fetal position and fell sound asleep.

Five

Detective Tommie Lane stepped away from her desk and to the nearest coffee machine. It was her fourth cup and she still had six hours left in her shift. This wasn't the first time she had worked twenty-four hours straight, but this time she was working on a special case and she and her team were close to finding what they believed to be a serial killer that was terrorizing spiritual leaders in Greensboro and the surrounding Piedmont Triad area.

Five victims later, they had dubbed him the *Holy Roller Bandit.* The HRB targeted well-known women who were members and leaders of prominent area churches. The first three women, first ladies of the area's largest churches, were brutally raped and left for dead—the last two had been raped and murdered. Tommy knew the sooner they had this crazy man off the streets, the better. They couldn't afford another death.

The women were mostly figures of non-denominational and Pentecostal churches—the ones that donned elaborate tailor made suits, large charismatic hats and glittery five-inch pumps. Each woman had some form of prolific position in her church, whether it was a minister's, pastor's or bishop's wife, deaconess or deacon's wife or even evangelist or melodic soloist. Tommie was familiar with them all.

At each crime scene, the suspect would leave a crisp pocket sized bible. The inscription left in each read, *He without sin. ~~Judge.*

Tommie was certain she and her team were closer to catching the culprit. The HRB had left something more than a bible at his last crime screen. In typical O.J.-like fashion, he had left behind one of his gloves. The glove was a blue exam glove that doctors and nurses used. Tommie was positive that forensics would find some sort of DNA on the biggest break they had.

One of the local pastors was due to head up a conference in Charlotte later in the week and Tommie and her fine team at the Greensboro Police Department were sure the HRB would use this as an opportunity to strike. And when he did, they would be ready. The killer was becoming sloppier by the moment.

“Yo, T.L., heads up,” Tommie’s partner, Detective John Sykes said. Tommie looked up just in time to catch a greasy Dunkin Donuts bag. Tommie had dozed off while reading reports from the case. She had sat in the same place for hours trying to find something in the report that would stand out.

“You’re still in the same place I left you. Figured I’d bring you a bite to eat,” Detective Sykes said.

“Thanks,” Tommie responded, frowning at the bag. She had sworn off unhealthy foods years ago. Although she had been on the force nearly fifteen years, she hadn’t always been in picture perfect health. She barely made it through the academy—lucky for her she knew someone, who knew someone. When she first joined the force, her five-foot-six frame weighed in excess of two-hundred pounds. She had been the target of daily taunting.

“Who’d you sleep with to get on the force?” she was asked one day after joining the team.

“Your mother,” she responded. “And that’s because sleeping with your father would have been too repulsive.” From day one, she had let those hot shots know that even though she couldn't run with the big dogs, she could most certainly hang with them. And, even though she had given up fast foods, it wasn’t until five years ago, that she decided that she would take care of herself and get into shape.

Her father, Captain Euless Lane, was the Chief of Police for the department. He was a thirty-year veteran and had gotten a bit too comfortable in his own skin. Tommie had begged her father to take better care of himself after he suffered a mild heart attack. He gave her plenty of lip service and never bothered to follow through.

After the first heart attack, Captain Lane did take better care of himself . . . that was until he thought he was out of the woods. Then, he stopped his minimal exercise program and started heavily eating fast food and drinking soda again. He eventually turned up the volume on his alcohol consumption, and then five years ago, an off-duty cadet found Captain Lane unconscious in his unmarked squad car during a murder investigation. At first glance, it was thought that he been killed by one of the suspects he was pursuing, but the medical examiner later confirmed that Captain Lane had died of a massive heart attack.

Tommie took her father's death hard, and from that point on, she swore that she would take better care of herself. She executed a strict exercise regimen and became a vegetarian. She had lost weight and turned her body into a lean muscle machine. And, although she fed her occasional cravings for Taco Bell, she still managed to eat healthy most of the time.

In fact, Tommie had made several changes in her life. Although she attended church on a regular basis, she was never one to be overly spiritual, but after years of being angry with God, she had finally turned her life over to Him and joined Destiny Christian Chapel.

Her mother had been murdered fifteen years earlier by her long-time boyfriend and Tommie blamed God. Her mother had no business with that man, but no one could tell her anything. All that mattered was that she had a man and she claimed she was in love. That man ended up *loving* her to death.

Tommie fell into a deep depression and almost hit rock bottom before being invited to a revival service one night. After a while, she was able to forgive the man that had taken her mother's life and she was able to forgive God, while asking and receiving His forgiveness. Her mother's killer was tried by a jury of his peers and ultimately received ninety-nine years in prison. It was then that Tommie decided to join the force. In addition to following in her father's footsteps, she wanted to give a voice to victims like her mother.

"So what do we have?" John asked her, focused on the police board. Filling from the large jelly donut he was eating rested on his uniform shirt.

"Well, we've been working with some of the more affluent pastors in the community. And, it's so tough. So far, we know that seven ministers in the Triad area will be leaving town within the next two weeks—two of who will be taking their wives." That was two less victims they had to worry about.

"So that means, the others will need security detail," John stated.

John had been Tommie's partner for a few years and she had considered them a close-knit team. John would tease her, calling her his second nagging wife, because Tommie always got on John about his health. John was an overweight Italian man who stood five-foot-six inches and weighed nearly three-hundred pounds. On the beat, he found himself out of breath often, but that didn't stop him from stuffing his face with unhealthy food choices. The precinct housed a gym, but John never found his way to it.

John was ten years older than Tommie and had been on the force longer—twenty-one years. Married to wife Sophia for thirty-three years, the two had three children—two sons and one daughter. John and his wife had used their life savings to pay for their oldest son's education; refinanced their mortgage for their daughter's education, and now, they had no idea where they'd get the money for their youngest child's education. John Jr. was smart, but not smart enough to receive a scholarship, but smart enough to get accepted to Stanford and Duke Universities.

The Sykes were backwards in their mortgage. And due to John's failure to keep up the home's maintenance, everything was falling apart. In the past, John found himself being able to work extra shifts at the precinct, but the election of North Carolina's new governor,

Pat McCrory, coupled with governmental cuts, John was lucky that he was able to work his regular shift at the precinct. Others with less seniority weren't so lucky. They had to take four furlough days a month in order to ward off budget costs and to keep their jobs.

Although she trusted him, Tommie didn't trust him completely. She always felt he was out to prove something. Even though he was her partner, she kept an eye on him. She knew things about him that he had no idea anyone knew. But, Tommie being the detective she was, knew how to keep things to herself—for as long as she needed.

"I have about seventeen more churches to call," Tommie said as she threw a sheet of paper at John. "You call half of these and I'll knock out the other half."

"You've got it," Detective Sykes said. The two got busy calling churches and setting up security detail in an effort to keep the women safe and catch the HRB.

Six

Tiffany was awakened by the sunlight coming through the skylight in the ceiling of her bedroom. It seemed as if she had just dozed off. She stretched and stared at the ceiling for a moment to collect her thoughts. She had a long day ahead of her and needed to gather her bearings. Even though she was set financially, Tiffany owned two businesses—one a non-profit and one a for-profit start-up.

Her non-profit, Womenpreneur of the Triad, was an organization that recognized and assisted women entrepreneurs in the Piedmont-Triad, who volunteered in the community and hired women from within the community, while trickling dollars back into the local economy. Of her entrepreneurial ventures, she was most passionate about this one.

She had a meeting with a group of sponsors for their upcoming *It Takes an Entrepreneur to Lead the Community Conference* that was being hosted in Greensboro this year. It was being held at the illustrious Grandover Resort. Even though she could afford to foot the bill herself, Tiffany believed in spending *other* people's money.

Her second love was Jordan Marketing Agency. She had started the agency while still married to Richard. She'd always had a creative side and after a fancy dinner party with a few of Richard's business associates and their wives, she decided she wasn't going to waste her blessing. She talked with Richard later that night and they agreed that if she could show him samples of packages that she might provide to clients at various stages of their business and finance level, he would front the start-up money and he would even let her retain one hundred percent ownership. She couldn't refuse that offer.

By the end of the next day, she had presented her husband with five marketing packages—from the thriftiest of clients to the most expensive. Richard was impressed beyond belief. He had always teased her telling her that she had used the three-thousand dollar creative Adobe Design software as an excuse to spend his money. She assured him that three-thousand dollars was chump change to him and one day he'd eat his words. He had no idea that she was teaching herself how to use every aspect of the software. The photos, mock advertisements, and print ads she had created, along with fancy budget spreadsheets, magazine layouts and media campaigns were none like he had seen before.

"You do realize you could work for one of the major brands, like McDonald's, Nike, Coke . . ."

"Why would I work for them when I could work for myself? Soon they'll all be asking for my expertise."

Richard had laughed and told his overzealous wife that although he loved her ambition, she was way out of her league. She would show him. Because Richard was always out doing his dirt or too busy with business to notice his wife, he hadn't noticed that she had picked up clients like Panera Bread, Costco, TJX Companies, which owns TJ Max, Marshalls and Home Goods, and her biggest, General Motors. She was excited when after three days of meeting with marketing executives at the large corporation, she received a FedEx package that enclosed a lucrative agreement with the company. All it needed was her signature. She had signed it on the spot and gave it right back to the delivery guy.

She was so excited, that she called Richard and told him that she wanted to celebrate her biggest deal to date. Of course, Richard's response was, "I'm sorry honey, I have to work late." That evening, she used her Verizon Wireless Family Tracker to track down the location of Richard's phone. It led her right to his mistress's home, the one he had paid for.

When Tiffany rang the doorbell, a short and stocky woman answered the door. She had a dark complexion and wore a pink silk robe. She knew immediately that it came from Nordstrom. Richard had bought her one just like it a few months earlier. When she reminded him that it was not her birthday, Richard told her he had seen it when he had gone shopping for a tie and thought about her the moment he saw it. She was sure Richard had bumped his head because she knew Richard never did any of his own shopping. But she remained silent, more ammo for her when she finally decided to file for divorce.

The woman that stood before her had to be in her late twenties and was of average beauty . . . and she was pregnant. There were no questions to be asked or answered, although she had never seen *this* woman before, she knew that the baby she carried was Richard's.

"Can I help you," the young girl asked politely.

"Yes, I'm looking for Richard Jordan. I'm Melissa, his assistant." Tiffany held out a legal sized envelope. "He's been waiting for these documents and instructed me to get them to him as soon as they arrived.

"I'll see that he gets them," the young lady offered.

"Please, I really want to deliver them myself. As I've said, he has been waiting for these legal documents for ages. I really want to see the expression on his face when he sees that his dreams have finally become reality."

The young lady agreed. For something this important, surely she could disturb her Sugar Daddy. "Richard! Honey, I've got good news for you," the young girl yelled out.

"What is it?" Tiffany heard Richard yell.

"The news you've been waiting for is finally here. Your assistant wanted to deliver the news herself." The young girl was excited. She was sure that whatever the news was, it was about more money for her and her unborn child. She nearly dragged Richard to the door, but stopped when Richard mumbled, "Oh shit."

"What is it honey?" she asked him.

"Well dear," Tiffany started. "Honey here is my husband. Aren't you *honey*?" she asked Richard. "But not for long," she said winking at her infidel of a husband.

"Baby, I can explain," Richard started, while the unsuspecting mistress looked on in disbelief.

"No need to, *honey*. Here are the papers you've been waiting for, for ages." Tiffany had overheard Richard tell one of his other mistresses that he couldn't wait to divorce the money hungry Mrs. Jordan.

"What is this?" Richard asked taking the envelope from her.

"Consider yourself served, you son-of-a-bitch." Tiffany turned to walk away but turned back to face the poor woman that now had a horrifying look on her face.

"Oh and sweetie, trust me when I say, you are not the only one. At least you were smart enough to trap him with a pregnancy. But I assure you, after I'm done with this bastard, your child won't see a penny of child support." Tiffany left the two with their jaws wide opened, jumped into her Range Rover and drove away.

Tiffany finally looked over at her cell phone that lay on the nightstand next to her bed.

She could barely sleep last night and the unknown caller was insistent upon keeping her up.

Tiffany gasped at the time. Her meeting was in ten minutes. She called her office and told her assistant to contact the sponsors to let them know her eta was twenty-minutes. Considering she was still lying in her bed, she had just told a lie.

Tiffany jumped out of bed and into the shower. She was out in five minutes flat. She threw on an old stand-by black pants suit and gold shell. She pulled her hair back into a ponytail, put on a coat of mascara and a dab of lip-gloss. After stepping into her patent leather pumps, she grabbed a strand of pearls from the dresser, ran down the stairs, grabbed her purse from the foyer and was out the door.

Fifteen minutes later, she exited the elevator on the twelfth floor and entered her office suite. Her secretary nodded towards her office door and whispered, "They've only been here for five minutes, so you should be okay. I've made sure they have coffee and water."

That was a relief for Tiffany. One thing she hated was being late and she didn't like it when others were late either.

Tiffany had made a great impression on her investors and sponsors. By the time the meeting had ended, Tiffany had secured thirty-two thousand dollars for the conference. In addition, she had secured a forty-five thousand dollar scholarship for her winning nominee. This brought her total to one-hundred-ten thousand dollars—slightly short of her one-hundred-fifteen thousand dollar goal. She felt pretty good about the meeting. In exchange for their money, she promised the sponsors an extensive marketing run in all their promotions. Marketing—something else she was good at.

Tiffany thought about Tommie and dialed her cell number.

"Detective Lane," Tommie answered.

"Hey darlin', what's up with you?" Tiffany asked.

"Hello beautiful. Same old, same old. Still trying to catch this mad man before he strikes again."

"I know with you on the job, you're sure to find him soon."

"From your mouth to God's ears. So what's going on your way?"Tommie asked her friend.

"Trying to get this conference off the ground and was wondering if you had time for lunch—or dinner."

"I thought we already bought our tickets."

"Oh girl, that's not what I wanted to talk to you about."

"Oh. How about Lucky 32 at one-thirty?" Tommie asked.

"Sounds like a plan. I have some things to tie up around here and I'll meet you there."

"See you in a bit," Tommie said and disconnected the line. Tiffany hated when Tommie did that. She never said goodbye.

Seven

Tiffany was waiting in the front lobby of the Lucky 32 restaurant when Tommie arrived. The two ladies hugged each other and exchanged pleasantries.

"God, you need to take better care of yourself," Tiffany told Tommie as she stood back to take a look at her friend. Tommie was wearing a pair of grungy jeans, a black t-shirt that read Greensboro Police Department in white letters across the front, and a pair of dusty, black combat boots. Her hair was pulled back into a ponytail and she wore no make-up. Tiffany knew under all the hardness of her job lied beautiful and sexy woman.

"Everyone can't wear designer suits like you, Ms. Divorcée," Tommie teased. She took in her friend's black pantsuit and simple pearls. Tiffany always looked flawless and with little effort. "Besides, I'm a cop. I'm not trying to impress anyone. I clean up good when I have to."

"Maybe if you made yourself more presentable, more often, you'd find a man," Tiffany mumbled as their waitress escorted them to their table. "And this is not a designer suit. I got it at White House Black Market, and it only cost $250."

"Well excuse me. And, I don't need a man—I'd just end up divorced, just like you," she teased.

Tiffany rolled her eyes. "But at least you'd be able to afford designer suits," she laughed. Tommie couldn't help but laugh too.

After the two ladies had placed their orders, Tommie leaned into Tiffany and asked, "So, what's really going on with you?"

"Well, I don't know if it's much of anything, but I haven't been sleeping well lately. You know how part of your psyche accepts something as normal, but your sixth sense tells you something is wrong? Well my psyche and my sixth sense have been having a battle lately."

"Why? What's going on with you?"

"I don't know. I've been hearing these noises in the house, and I have to say, they have me a bit on edge."

"I told you not to buy that big ol' house. Who does that?" Tommie asked, throwing her hands in the air. "You just had to go and prove a point to Richard didn't you. Richard is not thinking about you."

Tiffany cringed and gave Tommie the look.

"Well maybe he is, since you left him broker than a joker," Tommie added.

Tiffany rolled her eyes.

"That big ol' house is just settling in," Tommie said, easing up off her friend.

"That's what I thought at first. But, it's almost as if someone is watching me. There are even times when I feel like someone's in the same room as me. And if that isn't creepy. I'll put something somewhere, only to find it moved when I go back for it later. Tommie, please tell me that I'm not losing my mind. I'm too young and beautiful to be going senile."

"Well, I thought you lost your mind long before now—like when you bought that house," Tommie answered.

Tiffany rolled her eyes. She was so sick of Tommie ranting about her house. It was no secret that Tommie worked in law enforcement because she wanted to. Everyone knew that she had enough loot that would set her for the rest of her life. It wasn't like she couldn't afford a large home of her own, but she chose her small townhouse.

"But in all seriousness," Tommie continued, I think it's just the house. And, maybe you're just getting a bit forgetful. Look, you're a very busy woman and it's not uncommon to let things slip when you have so much going on."

"Well, I thought that too, until one day when I came home. I had to use the bathroom really bad. You know I never use the guest bathroom, I normally go upstairs to my master bath. This time, I couldn't make it up the stairs, so I used the one off the foyer. As I sat down, I fell into the toilet," Tiffany explained.

Tommie burst out in laugher, and then presumed her straight face. The visual of her supercilious friend falling into a toilet used by someone else brought tears to her eyes.

Tiffany raised an eyebrow and curled her lips.

"Why do you suppose I fell into the toilet?"

"The seat was up?"Tommie's investigative instincts set in.

"Right. And the last time that bathroom was even used was during our girl's weekend last month. Now, unless one of you failed to tell me you pee standing up . . . "

"How long have you been having these . . . episodes . . . these happenings?" Tommie interrupted. She had her thinking cap on now and had to admit that the toilet incident was a bit odd. She knew her friend Tiffany—she was a stickler about not using the same toilet as general population, including her friends. She knew that Tiffany wouldn't use that toilet unless she absolutely had to. Now Tommie was curious as to how that toilet seat was lifted and wanted to know as much as Tiffany did, about the odd happenings in the Jordan household.

"Well, actually, it's been going on for almost two months now."

"Two months? And you're just now saying anything?"

"Well at first, I thought it was just due to the fact that I'm alone in that big house. But then I started getting hang up calls on the landline and then my cell." Tiffany's eyes rolled down to the right and stayed there for a moment. "You know, I've gotten flowers; twice, from a secret admirer and everyone I talk to swears they didn't send them."

"We can talk to the flower shop to see who sent them—get a warrant if we need to," Tommie offered.

"No need," Tiffany interjected. "I called and the owner said the person was a male. He didn't give his name and paid with a pre-paid debit or gift card."

"Did he give you a description of the man?"

"He said he was a black man with a light complexion, about five-foot-eight. Oh, he said he had this strange bump in the middle of his forehead."

Tommie strained her face as Tiffany relayed to her what the owner of the flower shop had said. She didn't know why, but that description didn't sit well with her.

"What's wrong?"Tiffany asked her.

"I'm not sure why yet, but I'll sure let you know when I do." Tommie's mind was going a mind a minute. "Which flower shop was this?"

"Bonnie Brae?" Tommie asked. She had never heard of that flower store, at least not in the Triad.

"Yes. Bronnie Brae is a flower shop in Denver. That's where they were sent from."

"Colorado?"

"Yes. I was surprised too. I tried to think who would send me flowers from Denver. Since we graduated, I've only returned home a few times—once for a business trip and twice when we had the girl's weekend at Jillian's.

Tiffany knew her friends mind was rolling a mile a minute and she knew she was on to something. She also knew Tommie wasn't going to let her know what it was until she was sure.

"I'm going to follow you home, go through the house and make sure the locks and windows are secure."

"What are you thinking?" Tiffany asked her in a worried tone.

"I don't know yet. I have work to do."

Eight

Tommie followed her friend home, noting her surroundings. She kept a hand-held recorder with her so she could record those observations and her thoughts so she could use them at a later time.

"Gated community," Tommie stated into the recorder. "Two unarmed security personnel at the gate. Both Caucasian. Both in uniform and with radios. Both male. Gate took approximately seventeen seconds to fully open. Gates stayed open approximately thirty-three seconds and took approximately fifteen seconds to close. Ten-inch stone and brick walls on each side of the gates. A two-inch space in between gate and stone. Well kept neighborhood. Amount of cars in driveways indicative of upper echelon and working class. No children observed with the exception of one woman walking child in stroller by lake and two teenagers washing car by what appears to be the clubhouse. Lawn care personnel at one of the homes."

Tommie continued to follow Tiffany up the driveway of the enormous home.

"Home is a two-and-a-half to three-story with brick, stone and siding exterior. Two-car garage in front, but on right of home. Neatly landscaped yard, with flowers, bushes and approximately eighteen trees. Approximately two-hundred to three-hundred feet between left exterior of house and next house and approximately two-hundred to two-hundred-fifty feet from right exterior and next house. Back of house appears to be wooded. Entire parameter of home fenced with black wrought iron gate, with the exception of driveway and garage area."

Tommie was startled when Tiffany knocked on her car window. "Are you getting out?" Tiffany asked.

"Sorry, I was taking inventory of the area." She got out of her car and followed Tiffany through the garage. Tommie stopped for a moment and counted how long it took the garage door to close.

"Approximately twelve seconds for garage door to open and close," she spoke into the recorder.

Tiffany knew that having a friend on the police force could come in handy, but Tommie was starting to worry her.

Both women walked into the house and Tiffany shut the door behind them.

"Interior door opens into the laundry room, which opens into the kitchen." Tommie took several photos of Tiffany's house as she continued to talk into the recorder.

Tiffany watched her friend do what she did so well, but in the back of her mind, she couldn't help but think about earlier when she first expressed her concerns. Tommy seemed pretty laid back until Tiffany told her of the florist's description of her secret admirer. If she knew Tommie well enough, she knew her friend was keeping something from her. She retrieved two bottles of water from the fridge and joined her friend who had made her way up the staircase to the second level.

When Tiffany rounded the staircase and made her way down the hallway, she stopped at her bedroom door. Tommie was standing at the window, taking several photos with her cell phone.

"Did you find something Dr. Sleuth?"

Tommie was in detective mode. "When was the last time you opened this window?" She asked ignoring her friend's question.

"I don't know. Maybe when I first bought the house. I really don't open any of the windows, unless you count the one in my office and the one in the kitchen. I do open the patio doors downstairs often."

"Which one? The office or the great room?"

"Both. Why?"

"So then you didn't know that the lock on this window was broken?"

Tiffany brushed past Tommie to inspect her friend's findings. She was sure that she and the inspector had gone through the house when it was first built, and she knew the lock was not broken. Tiffany stood silent for a moment. She was speechless. She made a note to get the lock fixed when she got a chance. She followed Tommie to her walk-in closet.

"When was the last time you checked this window?" Tommie asked.

"Never. I've never used it. The skylight provides enough light for me in here, and if not, I have the chandelier."

"This lock is unlocked," Tommie said sternly. Tiffany could see that her friend was becoming very irritated and the last thing she wanted to do was irritate Tommie.

"Hey John, it's TL. Any messages for me?" Tommie spoke into her cell phone.

"No, you taking off?" her partner answered.

"Just a couple of hours. I have a personal issue I need to deal with. I'll talk to you about it later—I may need your help. I have my cell on me." The two talked shop for a few more moments before Tommie hit end and dialed another number.

Tiffany became nervous when she realized Tommie was talking to a locksmith.

"Yes, 27 Flagship Cove." There was silence before she heard Tommie speak again. Tommie explained to the locksmith what she needed and set an appointment. Afterwards, Tommie went through Tiffany's home with a fine-toothed comb. By the time she was done, the two were pooped and hungry.

"I can whip up dinner for us," Tiffany offered.

"No, I want you to order take-out," Tommie interjected. "What kind of take-out do you normally order?"

"Hmm . . . A few places on Pigsah. Oh and this great Mexican restaurant."

"I want you to place an order. One for the Mexican place and then another for the Chinese take-out place."

Tiffany looked at Tommie puzzled.

"Just do it," Tommie demanded as she lost herself in her thoughts.

After Tiffany had placed orders for both Chinese and Mexican, she needed answers.

"I've been quiet most of the day and you have me scared to death. Are you going to tell me what's going on?"

"How long is it going to take for the food?"

"Twenty to thirty minutes. You still haven't answered . . . " was all Tommie allowed Tiffany to get out.

"Where is your attic and any crawl spaces or vents you have going into and out of the house? Once I've documented that, I'll tell you what I think over dinner."

Tiffany was happy with that answer—for now. She escorted Tommie to the attic where the crawl space was but refused to go into it with her. After she didn't hear from her friend after five minutes, she called up to her.

"Tommie. Is everything okay in there?"

"No, but I don't want you to come in here."

"Why not?"

"Just wait for me. I'll be out in a minute."

Moments later, Tommie emerged from the large crawl space.

"Do you have a padlock around here somewhere?" she asked.

Tiffany was starting to get a bit concerned. "Yes, why?"

"Just get it."

When Tiffany returned with the padlock, complete with key, she handed it to Tommie and watched as she secured the crawl space. The two ladies made their way downstairs just as the doorbell rang.

"You get that and act as you normally would," Tommie instructed Tiffany. Tommie hid in the nook in the foyer as Tiffany opened the door.

"Hola Senorita Tiffany," the delivery man greeted her.

"Hola Senor Hector. Do you ever get a day off?" Tiffany asked trying to make small talk.

"Well when your family owns the restaurant, vacations are few and far between senorita. Besides, I don't mind. I love what I do and I get all the free Mexican food I want." They both laughed.

I guess you have a point there," Tiffany agreed.

"I have your usual, smothered chimichanga, with extra jalapenos."

"Gracias Hector," Tiffany thanked him as she gave him a tip. The two spoke a couple more pleasantries before Hector was off to his next delivery.

"Does he always stay at the door?" Tommie asked.

"Yes, I never let them in the house. You should know that."

"Does he know you live alone?"

"I'm not sure. I've never mentioned it, but I gather he could probably figure that out since I only order for one each time I order. That, and the fact that I'm the one that always opens the door."

The doorbell rang again and Tiffany sat the Mexican take-out on the foyer table as Tommie hid once more.

"Hello," Tiffany said when she opened the door.

The Asian delivery man bowed to Tiffany and said, "Hewo." He was one of three delivery men from the Chinese restaurant that Tiffany could remember.

"House . . . A . . . Fry rice and . . . Mongolian chicken . . . And hot a sour soup . . . And crab a won ton," the delivery man recited her order.

"Thank you so much," Tiffany replied, taking the bag of food and giving the delivery man a tip. The man bowed to Tiffany once more and thanked her before he pranced back to his vehicle. Tiffany shut the door and handed the bag of food to Tommie. Both ladies with food in tow, headed to the kitchen.

Once they had food on their plates and wine in their glasses, Tommie finally spoke. "Someone's been in your house."

Tiffany nearly choked on her glass of wine. "What?"

"The crawl space looks like someone's been living up there. That explains why you have broken locks on your windows."

"You've got to be kidding me Tommie, this is not funny."

"It shouldn't be. You said you've been getting an eerie feeling. It's because someone has been watching you. Are you and Richard getting along well?"

"Honestly, I haven't talked to Richard in weeks." Tiffany thought back to her last conversation with Richard. He had moved on. The divorce was bitter, but she was certain that Richard couldn't be the one that was . . . stalking her. She was sure that Richard didn't even know where she lived. She used a post office box for mail delivery. She supposed if he really wanted to find out where she lived, he could. He did know people in high and low places.

"Are you dating anyone, or do you know of anyone that you may have pissed off?"

"Not that I can think of. How in the hell can someone be in my house and I not know?"

"I've been wondering the same thing," Tommie said. Tiffany had always been a little flighty and in her own world.

The two continued to eat and devised a plan to make sure Tiffany's house was more secure. Tommie insisted that Tiffany stay at her place for the night. She'd make sure all the locks were changed and the broken ones were fixed. Then they'd make sure they upgraded her security services with ADT.

"Let me give Jillian a call. If those flowers came from Denver, then maybe she knows someone that may have a crush or something on you. That may explain the flowers, but honestly, that's the least of our worries. I'm more concerned about the fact that someone has been entering and leaving your house without your knowledge."

"Truth be told Tommie, I'm rarely home, except to sleep most times. Hell, there are parts of this house I've never been in since I bought it." Tiffany stopped, because she knew the look on Tommie's face. It was the one that often said she should have never bought the big house that was too big for her in the first place. But Tommie knew her friend got the message and chose not to say anything.

When Tommie dialed Jillian's number, she got her voice mail, so she chose to leave a message. "Hey Jillian, it's Tommie."

"And Tiffany!" Tiffany yelled into the phone.

Tommie continued, "Just calling to chat with you. Hope all is well. Get back with us. We need to get details finalized for our next girl's weekend here in the next couple of weeks. Love you, bye." Tommie ended the call and she and Tiffany continued eating their food and talked about the happenings at 27 Flagship Cove.

Nine

When Tommie returned to the precinct, she was greeted by Detective Sykes.

"Is everything okay?" he asked.

"Actually no. Tiff has a stalker and he has managed to hide out in her house."

Detective Sykes stopped for a minute before saying, "Oh no, did you catch the creep?"

"Unfortunately . . ." Tommie started.

"Well I hate to ruin your day, but HRB has struck again," John interrupted her.

"The Holy Roller Bandit?" Tommy didn't think she could take any more. She wanted to catch this lunatic before he had struck again, but she had failed. She also made a mental note of the detectives reaction to her findings.

"Where?" she asked him.

"Grace and Mercy on Lee."

"First Lady Simmons?" she inquired.

"Actually no. I believe his target was Mrs. Simmons, but she had to go out of town last minute. He got the assistant pastor this time."

"Pastor McCullough," Tommie sighed, more so, a statement than a question. Since the case had begun, she made it a point to learn nearly every clergy in the Piedmont Triad. That included Greensboro, High Point, Winston-Salem, Burlington, Kernersville and a few other Piedmont Triad cities.

She sat down at her desk and studied the vicinity board. She tried to figure out if there was pattern and if she could tell where the killer would strike next.

"Have we received ballistic and DNA reports?" she asked John.

"Yes, the ballistics from the last incident come back to a gun that was reported stolen. Get this, the gun was reported stolen from Atlanta three months ago."

"So our perp has a connection between Atlanta and North Carolina?"

"Yes, and that's not it. We checked out the printer for those bibles. We traced them back to a company in Dallas. They said that someone by the name of Paige Guillory ordered two hundred and fifty of them and had them shipped to Atlanta."

Tommie froze for a moment. She couldn't put her finger on it, but that meant something to her. "Guillory . . . Guillory . . . ?" Tommie repeated to herself. "Why does that name sound so familiar?" Tommie sat in her chair and took a sip of the cold coffee that sat on her desk. "She must have paid by credit card, did we get a hit?"

"A no go TL. It was one of those prepaid debit cards. You can get them anywhere, like your local Wal-Mart or Walgreen's. You don't need an ID to purchase them."

Tommie went over notes trying to put some clarity to the case. It was getting crazier by the moment.

"We got the DNA results back too?" Tommie asked her partner.

"Not last I checked. The lab said something about the substance found inside the glove may make it harder to get a good DNA sample. But I'll head to the lab to see if they have any new information."

"John," Tommie said, not looking up from her notes.

"Yeah TL?"

"Do you think it's possible that we have a cross country serial killer?"

"Nah, I doubt it," Detective Sykes said.

This caused Tommie to look up from her files. The John Sykes she knew would have at least entertained the thought.

When her partner couldn't maintain eye contact with his suspecting partner, he broke the awkward silence. "I'll be in the lab," he said and then turned and walked away.

Tommie watched as her friend disappeared into the stairwell. She had noticed that her friend had been acting strange as of late, but she couldn't put her finger on it. She shook her head and dove back into her files.

Once in the stairwell, Detective Sykes pulled out his cell phone. "What's my next step?" he asked the voice on the other end.

"Were you able to take care of our little problem?" the unidentified man asked.

"Yes. I mixed a few of the samples in the lab together and added ammonia for effect."

"Good. Good. You keep me up to date on that process. I want to be certain that the DNA from that glove cannot be traced back to me. In the meantime, I've left the Greensboro Police Department a little gift."

"A gift?" Detective Sykes asked. Before he could say anything else, his cell phone went dead. The detective soon found out exactly what Lucien meant when he returned to the squad room.

Captain Randall and Tommie were looking at the investigative board. Detective Sykes joined them.

"What are we looking at?" he asked them.

"We've got another one," Tommie answered still observing a board.

"Where?"

"High Point Piedmont Christian," Captain Randall said.

Detective Sykes lowered his head. His mystery friend had been very busy. He wondered how many more had to suffer; how many more had to die for the cause.

When Tommie finally turned to face her partner, his face and neck were beet red. "You okay John?" she asked him.

"Yes, why do you ask?"

"If you were any redder, you'd catch fire."

"I feel fine. It is a little warm in here. Are we headed out to the scene?" he answered.

"Yes, grab your gear," Tommie ordered as she grabbed her bag and headed out of the station. Captain Randall watched the two from his office window. He, too, had noticed that Detective Sykes had been acting a bit odd in the past few weeks.

Ten

Detectives Lane and Sykes arrived on the scene at High Point Piedmont Christian Center. Several officers, investigative and forensics teams were already on top of things. They both entered the church and started their observation.

"Who would do this?" a young lady in her twenties screamed out. Tommie walked over to her to comfort her and to see if she could get any information.

"This is the daughter of First Lady Tarrant," one of the officers told her before leaving the two alone.

"Hi sweetie, what's your name?" Tommie asked the horrified woman.

"Monica. Monica Tarrant. Who would do this to my mother? Why?" she asked, crying uncontrollably.

"Tell me what you know if you can," Tommie said.

"I don't know anything!" the girl screamed.

"Calm down. I'm here to help and you'd be surprised how you could help and not even know it. I'm going to have an officer take you outside. You don't need to be here right now." Tommie motioned for an officer to take the young lady out to one of the patrol cars.

Once the young lady was escorted out of the church, Tommie lifted the white sheet from the deceased woman and observed as much as she could. The woman saw her attacker. She was shot at point blank range in the forehead. Her emerald green hat, that matched her pricey tailored suite, laid next to her and covered her right arm and hand. Tommy lifted the hat to study the blood spatter pattern. When she lifted the hat, she saw the bible. And, just like at the others, the bible had the infamous HRB calling card . . . scripture. Tommie cringed. Anyone who used God for their own personal agenda was just plain sick. She knew they had to catch this maniac as soon as possible.

Tommie took more notes and photos while the forensic team before heading out to the church parking lot to speak with Monica Tarrant. As she headed toward the exit she heard a call go out over her radio. She removed the radio from her hip holster and listened to the call.

"Reported shots fired at 4322 Elmsley . . . New Life Pentecostal Church . . . possible 187 . . . multiple victims . . ." Tommie dropped to her knees and said a prayer. God had to give her the tools to stop this madness.

Detective Sykes ran into the church sanctuary. He was sweaty and out of breath. "A call just went out over the scanner. They're saying multiple injuries and possibly multiple deaths. We need to get over there now!"

"I will meet you there, I need ask Ms. Monica a few questions."

Detective Sykes didn't give Tommie time to say anything else. He was out of the church and into his squad car in a flash.

Tommie watched Monica who now stood next to one of the undercover patrol cars talking on her cell phone. The young lady was still hysterical. Tommie joined her and put her arms around her.

"I need you to answer a few questions so we can catch the person who did this to your mother. "

Monica nodded in between sobs. Tommie recorded the question and answers session with the young woman.

A few moments later a new model Mercedes drove up. An older, slim woman, dressed in a black tailored pantsuit, exited the silver sedan, ran towards Monica and took her into her arms. She extended her free hand to Tommie and explained that she was the deceased's sister. She volunteered to take Monica to her home until her father Pastor Tarrant returned home.

Tommie turned to give one last look at the church before heading off to the next crime scene.

Eleven

Tommie arrived on the scene at New Life Pentecostal. First responders and police personnel were everywhere. The church was one of the largest in the area and boasted a membership above ten thousand. She saw several victims being treated or being rushed off to local hospitals.

She had visited this church when she had first arrived in Greensboro. The church was too large for her to submit her membership, but she came back to visit often—when there was a collaborative revival, gospel concert or community effort.

Tommie entered the church lobby and took in the scene. Her heart stopped when she saw several sheet-covered bodies strewn about. From where she stood, she saw at least four and she knew once she stepped into the sanctuary, she would find more. It was obvious to her that mid-day Wednesday bible study was in session when the tragedy happened.

She took in the position of each body, spatter patterns, and the location of bullet entries. She examined each body and took notes with her handy recorder. One body in particular did not show any front entry wounds. She nudged the body onto its side and realized that the woman had been shot several times in the back. The blood spatter indicated that once the woman was shot, she fell backwards onto front desk before hitting the ground.

Detective Sykes made his way to the lobby. "You need to get in here as soon as possible. It looks like a complete massacre in there."

"Did you find the HRBs calling card?" Tommie asked him.

"No. It's possible this is not the HRBs doing. Follow me," he instructed Tommie.

Once inside the sanctuary, Tommie was horrified, there were bodies everywhere. Blood was splattered all over the large sanctuary and stage. There were men, women and children.

"Who did this?" she exclaimed.

Just then Captain Randall entered the sanctuary. "HRB," he said.

"But John says there was no calling card," Tommie said.

"We found it in the parking lot," Captain Randall said handing the bible to a forensic specialist for bagging.

"Captain, we've got to find this guy and we've got to find him now."

"I'll meet you two back at the station," the captain said nodding towards Detective Sykes. "Meet me there in twenty."

"What about this . . ."

"Let these guys do their job, we've got work to do. That's an order."

After taking a few more photos and a few more notes, Tommie and John headed towards the station. While in her car, Tommie dialed Tiffany's number.

"Hey Detective," Tiffany answered.

"Hey Darlin'," Tommie responded.

"What's up with you?" Tiffany asked.

"Have you watched the news at all today?

"No, why?

"The HRB has struck twice in one day. This last scene was horrific."

"Are you okay? How about I bring you something to eat? What can I do for you?"

"I'm fine, and thanks for being concerned. But I have to say, I don't feel comfortable with you staying in that house by yourself," Tommie expressed her concern.

"I thought you said HRB's targets churches."

"Yes, but I can't ignore what's being going on in your house. And I would not be able to live with myself knowing this could be the same guy and I left you unprotected."

"Tommie, I told you, I'm not leaving my house," Tiffany interjected.

"At least let me get you security detail," Tommie pleaded.

"No. Look, I thank you for looking you for looking out for me. But absolutely not. I will not live in fear."

"Fine, them I'm going to be bunking with you until we catch this creep."

"That's fine. I could stand the company. But you better not be late for dinner, or we're getting a divorce!"

The two ladies laughed and expressed their love for each other before Tommie ended the call without saying goodbye as usual.

Twelve

Tommie was surprised to see her partner sitting at his desk when she returned to the precinct. She had left New Life Church before he did.

"Any word from the lab on that DNA sample," Tommie asked him throwing her bag onto her desk.

"Not yet," Detective Sykes responded.

"What in the hell is taking them so long?" Tommie asked picking up her telephone. But her partner stopped her before she could dial.

"But get this. We traced the sequence numbers on that pre-paid credit card back to a Wal-Mart in Denver."

"Denver? Colorado?" Tommie nearly fell out of her chair.

"Yea," Detective Sykes answered. "What's up?"

Tommie didn't answer, but started surfing on her computer. After talking to Tiffany earlier in the day, this was too much of a coincidence. She searched the Colorado Department of Corrections website for inmate Lucien Guillory. She knew that last name sounded familiar. Could it be that Lucien had married while in prison and he now had a wife? A wife that was carrying on his legacy? What she saw next sent a wave of fear through her body. According to the Colorado Department of Correction's website, Lucien had been released nearly a year ago.

"How can this be?"

"What?" Detective Sykes asked. He wanted to know what had gotten his partner all riled up. He also wanted to know what she knew that he didn't, so he could stay one step ahead of her, and so that he could report back to the man that had hired him.

Tommie frantically searched Google for any news story that pertained to Lucien, while she dialed the number to the Department of Corrections in Limon, Colorado. She needed to find out why she hadn't been notified of Lucien's release.

Her heart sank when the clerk told her that several attempts were made to notify her, but none of the contact information they had on file was current. Tommie melted in her chair. She thanked the clerk, ended the call and continued googling Lucien Guillory. She found three current articles, one in particular stood out. It was accompanied by a photograph of Lucien in the courtroom when the judge overturned his conviction. He had a sinister smirk on his face.

"There is no way on earth," Tommie said to herself. She now saw the connection to Atlanta, Georgia, being that was where Lucien was originally from. She knew that Lucien's parents lived there also, but she hadn't had any contact, let alone thought about Lucien for fifteen years. She called down to the records and technology clerk and ordered a copy of Lucien's criminal history to be expedited to her office. How could the justice system let this man go?

After checking government and public records, Tommie discovered that Lucien's father had died shortly after Lucien was sentenced. When she found a last known address for his mother, she wrote the address down and called one of her law enforcement connections in Atlanta.

"Howdy Mike," she said into the receiver.

"The only black woman that I know who says howdy. This must be the infamous Tommie Lane. How the heck are you doing?"

Tommie chuckled. All her life she had tried to escape the "whitest black girl" label that she received in middle school. It had followed her well into adult hood, only now she was pegged as the "whitest black woman" people knew. Some had told her that her "black card" was being revoked. Truth be told, she never held that card.

"I'm doing good Mike, how are you? How are things there in Hotlanta?"

"Let's just say that it's the same as it was the last time we talked, only ten times worse. These people out here are crazy these days."

"They've been crazy, they've just gotten crazier," Tommie agreed.

"I hear you on that. So what can I do for the beautiful Ms. Lane? It is still Ms. isn't it?" he inquired.

"Yes it is. You know I'm married to my job," she laughed.

"Well, if you were married to me, you wouldn't have to be married to that job."

"And that's exactly why I'm married to my job," she laughed. Mike made it a point to flirt with Tommie every time they spoke. "Listen, what can you find out on a George and Mary Guillory?"

Mike searched his data base as Tommie fed him information. "Wow. George Guillory use to be the chief of police here. Small world isn't it?"

"Smaller than you think," Tommie responded.

"Okay, I'm showing that Major Guillory died about eight years back—a gang related shooting. Mary died a couple of years ago of breast cancer." Mike continued to type and then said, "Hey Tommie, let me guess. You're not really inquiring about George or Mary at all, are you? My guess is that what you really want is a profile on their son, Lucien." Mike was silent for a few seconds before he said, "Tommie, what's going on? Why are you asking for a sheet on the man that killed your mother?"

"What else does his file say?" Tommie asked.

"It says he was convicted of killing Barbara Ann in 1997 in which he received ninety-nine years."

"Go on," Tommie instructed.

Mike was silent for a moment as he continued reading Lucien's jacket. "Wait a minute. They overturned his conviction late last year. He's out?"

"Yes, and I think he may be the serial killer we're looking for in the Holy Roller Bandit case."

"You've been looking for him since he got out?" Mike asked.

"Actually, yes and no. Corrections in Colorado claimed they couldn't locate me when Lucien was released, so I had no idea he was out. It wasn't until a few moments ago when I start to put two and two together. But we think he has an accomplice. A woman by the name of Paige Guillory ordered the bibles that this idiot is leaving at each crime scene."

"I don't show any record of marriage on his jacket. Let me check the public records here in Georgia." Mike was quiet while he searched for marital records. "There's nothing on record here. You may want to check other states. I can either courier his jacket to you, or I can have records scan and fax them."

"I've experienced your records department. I'd probably get them faster if you sent them by camel," Tommie joked. Actually, she wasn't joking. Her experience with Atlanta's records department left a bad taste in her mouth.

"There's a young lady down there who's quite smitten by me," he laughed. "I'll have her do them and you'll have them in a few hours."

"Smitten? And they want to deny *me* a black card?" They both laughed. "Thanks for your help Mike, I appreciate it."

"Anytime Ms. Lane. And, the next time you're in the ATL, why don't you let me take you out to dinner. You know, show you a good time."

"I'll keep that in mind," Tommie said before hanging up the phone. "Fat chance," she mumbled to herself.

Thirteen

"How much longer is this going to last?" Detective Sykes asked the man on the other end of the telephone once he was safe in his car and out of the view of prying eyes.

"Until I have finished what I started," the male voice said.

"Well I suggest you work a little faster, she's starting to put two and two together."

"That's not possible. You said yourself that she didn't even know I was out."

"She didn't until about ten minutes ago."

"What the hell are you talking about John? Talk . . . Now!"

"Well your little girlfriend got a little careless. When she ordered those bibles, she used your last name. They were traced to a store there in Denver. And, that's the *least* of your worries. That little horror movie you left back at New Life has them more eager to capture you. And trust me, if I know Tommie Lane, she will get her man."

The mysterious man started to inform Detective Sykes that he was actually in Greensboro, but thought against it.

"Lucien, I suggest you stop this now and leave town, but not before paying me my money," the detective got a little loud and then lowered his voice. "I cannot continue to help you and have my team become suspicious."

"Dammit!" Lucien said before slamming his fist into a nearby table and ending the call.

Detective Sykes wiped his forehead. He knew he was in too deep. He had made a deal with the devil and there was no way he could get out of it. He had accepted an offer—one he couldn't refuse. Sure, he made a decent salary at the precinct, but he wanted to be able to send his third child to college. After spending the family savings and refinancing the house, the Sykes were struggling.

Even so, he knew everything about this was wrong. He had been Tommie's partner for over five years and now he was selling her up the river. He had to admit that he'd always been a little jealous, but even so, he held high regard for his partner and considered her one of his family. He had convinced himself, he wouldn't let things go too far. He would do what Lucien had asked, then, he would catch the Holy Roller Bandit and turn him in before his partner. Then he'd surely be considered for a promotion and his partner wouldn't get hurt in the process.

Detective Sykes watched Tommie from the coffee station as she talked on the phone and studied the crime board, pacing back and forth. She had one arm crossed across her mid-section, while her free hand held the phone. He wondered how he had worked with her this long and not notice how beautiful she actually was. Sure, he teased her about being his second wife, but at this moment, it was as if he had an epiphany.

Tommie's bronzed skin glowed when she was intense. He figured it was compliments of an African-American father and a Caucasian mother. She always kept her long, naturally wavy, auburn hair in a pony tail. She kept her nails short and never wore any makeup. She didn't really need it, she was naturally beautiful. She sort of reminded him of Angela Bassett—strong and beautiful. She was in great shape, but one couldn't tell, because she always wore khaki pants, and a police issued jacket, along with dark tennis shoes. John couldn't remember ever seeing Tommie in anything fancier than a black pant suit. He pictured her in a short, low cut red dress and a pair of five-inch Jimmy Choos. She shook his head and brushed off the fact that he was thinking of his partner in a way that the shouldn't.

He could tell Tommie was heavy in thought and he knew that as smart as she was, it was just a matter of time before she figured things out. He had to act fast and he needed to light a fire under Lucien Guillory.

He joined her at the board and offered her a cup of coffee just the way she liked it. Even though she had just topped off her coffee cup, she thanked him for the extra caffeine.

"Anything yet?"

"Yes, and I can't believe it, but I think . . ." Tommie stopped for a moment as if she was lost in thought. John studied her as a look of disbelief fell across his partners face.

"What is it?" he inquired.

"The DNA report came back from the lab," Tommie said.

Detective Sykes gulped and rubbed his hands together. He began sweating profusely, but tried to remain calm. He was ninety-nine percent sure that he had contaminated the evidence beyond recognition. It was the other one percent he wasn't so sure about.

"What were the results?" he asked nervously.

Tommie watched sweat drip from her partners forehead. He had become extremely clammy.

"Well let's just say that I'm almost positive that the Holly Roller Bandit is my former step-father. It appears the DNA results lead back to him and a few *other* people. The lab thinks that someone tried to sabotage the DNA sample. They found a chemical compound and other human cultures, but they were able to confirm one of those cultures."

John nearly choked on his coffee. "What?" He tried to clear his throat, but the coffee had found its way through his nasal passage. Even though he handled the specimen with gloves, he prayed that none of his DNA was found in any of those samples.

"Who is it?" Detective Sykes inquired again not sure he had heard her correctly. When he had asked Lucien his connection to Tommie, Lucien would only tell him that Tommie had testified against him, claiming that she was an eye witness to a crime he hadn't committed, and it cost him fifteen years in prison. He never once mentioned that he had a personal connection to Tommie.

"Step-father?"

"Yes. My mother and father never married, although they remained good friends. My mother used to be a medical supervisor at one of the clinics in Denver back in the late seventies. Lucien had come in to get stitches from a gunshot wound. I was little then, but I remember that, even then, he was trouble."

Detective Sykes leaned against Tommie's desk enthralled in Tommie's story.

"Lucien was awaiting trial for murder. He had been accused of killing a woman in his car. They say he stabbed her several times, but for some reason the case was dismissed because the evidence was only circumstantial. Back then, DNA wasn't as prominent as it is now, and even though they found blood in his car, they didn't have enough to convict. Even so, you'd think that would have been enough to make my mother run."

Detective Sykes could not believe what he was hearing.

"I'm a little confused. Why is your former step-father killing women in the Triad? Does he have a connection here? I mean is his family from around here?"

"Actually, his family is from Atlanta. I found out that his father was murdered years ago and his mother died two years ago from breast cancer. I remember my mother saying he had a couple of sisters, but I never met any of them."

"Wait, I'm still confused. Why . . ."

"In 1997," Tommie interrupted her partner, "he killed my mother. He killed her the same way he killed the other woman he was accused of killing, except, this time, he was caught in the act. He stabbed her twenty-six times."

Detective Sykes could barely breathe as he wondered what he'd gotten himself into. Lucien never mentioned any of the details he was hearing from his partner.

"How long were he and your mother together?" John asked.

"Nearly twenty-three years."

"Do you know what made him snap?"

"No one really knows. It was only a matter of time."

"What do you mean?" John inquired.

"Not to mention that he was acquitted for killing another woman, Barbara Ann and Lucien had a volatile relationship. For as long as I could remember, abuse was a big part of our everyday lives. For years, Lucien would beat my other on a whim. I can recall so many instances." Tommie looked off into space and began to reminisce.

"I remember one time so vividly. Lucien had come home from work drunk and he started beating my mother's head against the washing machine. She yelled for me to run and get help, but no one would. They had been so used to it, and after my mother continued to take him back, no one wanted to get involved. Anyway, I remember her running out of the house, there was blood all over her face.

"She grabbed my hand and told me to run. Lucien chased us three blocks to a busy intersection. He caught up with us and dragged my mother across the busy street. Instead of anyone stopping to help her, they honked their horns for them to get out of the way. Once he got her across the street. I remember him beating her head against a brick building. I believe it was Roy's Laundry.

"One of my mother's friends lived right down the street and I ran to her house to see if I could get help. Mae grabbed her gun and followed me back to where my mother and Lucien were. My mother was barely responsive and Lucien was still beating her. Oh, but he stopped real quick—as soon as he saw that revolver."

"You were watching all of this?" John asked in disbelief.

"Yes, but it wasn't the first time, and it certainly wasn't the last."

"Why do you think your mother stayed with him so long?"

"Who knows? I really think it was because he kept a roof over her head and he somewhat accepted a child that wasn't his. I think, somehow, she felt that was enough. That, and the fact that she could *say* she had a man in her life."

"Wow." John had sat down in a chair next to Tommie's desk.

"Yeah. But then things changed. My mother had contracted a lung disease around 1978. I forget what they called it then—fibrosis something—I think it's the equivalent to today's COPD. But she was in a coma for nearly a year and just when they were about to take her off life support, she came out of her coma." Tommie stood up and walked over to the crime board, but continued her conversation.

"It took her months to recover, but after she got better and came back home, Lucien promised he would never put his hands on her again—and he didn't. Well, not at least until 1997. But I think my mother was so used to that man beating on her that she didn't know how to act when he wasn't. It got to point that she started being the abuser. I guess he finally just snapped."

"Where was your father in all of this?"

"Here in Greensboro. My mother and father were never in a relationship. I think they caught each other at a vulnerable time—one time and that was all it took. But my father was already married and happened to be in Denver on a business trip when it happened. He never lost touch and always made sure I was always well taken care of."

"He didn't try to take you out of that environment?"

"He only knew about a few instances. I knew if I had told him everything, that he'd probably gain custody. But, I wasn't leaving my mother with that monster, so I never said much. Besides, she was my mother. My dad had another family and didn't have much time for me."

John's face was beet red as he tried to hold back tears. Tommie had shared a lot of herself with him, and he with her, but she had never gone this deep.

"Anyway," Tommie said, changing the mood and the subject, "let's go find this bastard before he kills again."

Fourteen

When Tiffany pulled into her driveway and lifted the garage, Tommie's black unmarked police-issued Chevy Tahoe was parked on the right hand side of the structure next to the Jaguar. She pulled into the empty space. She collected her purse and her briefcase and went inside.

"Honey, I'm home!" she said as she walked through the laundry room and into the kitchen.

"You're retarded Tiffany," Tommie laughed.

"I know," Tiffany agreed as she walked to the six burner stove, she rarely used and sniffed the aroma coming from one of the pots.

"Whatchu cooking?" she asked.

"My famous spaghetti," Tommie said.

"Spaghetti?"

"Yes, Ms. Lobster Tail. Try some common folk food every now and then."

"Tommie, why do you pretend you don't have as much money as I do, if not more?"

"Oh hush it, you booghatwa!"

"Booghatwa? What kind of word is that?" Tiffany asked.

"Don't act like you don't know what that word means."

Tiffany rolled her eyes at Tommie as she watched her best friend chop cloves of garlic. "You really think I'm bourgeois?"

"I think you're Tiffany and I love me some Tiffany."

Tiffany smiled and opened the oversized fridge. "I just know you went grocery shopping before you got here, because that food you're making and all this food in the fridge was not here when I left this morning. As a matter of fact, my fridge had *never* had that much food in it."

"Which goes to show, you probably shouldn't have bought that big fridge like you probably shouldn't have bought this big house," Tommie said.

"There you go," Tiffany said. "Is it safe to go upstairs *detective*? I need to get out of these clothes."

"Funny you are. Yes, I've swept the entire house from top to bottom. Hey I wanted to ask you, did it ever occur to you to install an intercom when you had the security system installed?"

"No, why?"

"Oh, I don't know," Tommie said sarcastically. "Maybe because you have three floors *and* a basement."

"Hmph," Tiffany retorted. "I'm shocked *you* haven't installed one *Detective* Lane."

"Ha. I got you. One is being installed tomorrow at eleven a.m."

"Why am I not surprised?" Tiffany asked as she made her way up the spiral staircase.

Tommie put the finishing touches on the spaghetti and sat at the kitchen island going over the files in the folder she had brought home from work. She tried to pin point where she'd thought the HRB would strike next, who was working him and what she had in common with the deceased. She lined up photos of all of the deceased on the counter and thought hard. She knew each of the women, they had all attended a women's conference together.

"Wait a minute," she said to herself. "We all attended the conference together. But why would Lucien have any interest in that?" She then turned to the jacket of information sent to her compliments of Mike at the Atlanta police department.

Upstairs, Tiffany slid out of her six-inch heels and rubbed her feet. She sat on the side of the bed, closed her eyes and fell back onto the bed. She had to catch a clear thought—or none at all. The Women's Expo was only three weeks away. She had tied most of the loose ends, but she was still going back and forth with the caterer on the final menu. Should she have duck or should she have salmon? Should she have pie or should she have crepes? Should she have . . . sweet tea? Where she was from it was just plain tea. You either drank it unsweetened or you asked for two Splendas or Equals. *Southerners*, she thought to herself.

She pulled out a t-shirt and a pair of leggings from her closet and jumped in the shower. Half way through her rinse cycle she heard a loud thump. She expedited her cleansing ritual and stepped out of the shower.

"Tommie?" she called out grabbing a towel and drying herself. There was no answer. She called for Tommie again, still no answer. That intercom system was sounding more and more attractive. Thank God for cell phones. She texted Tommie . . . *get up here now!*

Within seconds Tommie came running into the bedroom with her gun drawn. Tiffany shrieked. "Watch where you're pointing that thing!"

"I thought you were in distress. What happened?"

"I heard a loud thud. Is it thundering?"

"No. I didn't hear anything," Tommie said drawing her gun again, searching Tiffany's master suite before checking the attic.

Tiffany got dressed and followed her friend. She'd rather be behind her happy-gun-toting buddy instead of in front of her.

The two ladies checked every inch of the house. When they were sure that every nook and cranny was secure, the two retreated to the kitchen to eat their meal.

"You need to get better flood lights too. Make sure they're motion censored," Tommie said.

"First thing in the morning," Tiffany assured her.

Tommie poured them both a glass of wine. "Do you remember the conference we attended a while back?" she asked Tiffany.

"I've been to so many in the year or so, which one are you talking about?"

"The First Ladies Conference."

"Yes, the one where all the prominent first ladies in the area attended. I remember it. It was the one with Shirley Caesar. You know she's from Durham don't you?" Tiffany asked her.

"I had no idea."

"You've been here how long?"

"Anyway," Tommie continued as she went through the file jackets. "Every last one of the vics attended that conference, including you and I."

Tiffany looked at her with an element of surprise and after a moment of silence, she said, "Well we were all there. You, me, Kim, Jennifer and Jillian. Speaking of Jillian, has she returned your call?"

"No, but she sent me an email this morning said she didn't have time to call but she'd be down for the next girl's weekend."

"She was too busy to pick up the phone to call her best friends, but she wasn't busy enough to send an email?"

"Hey, she's *your* friend," Tommie said.

"She's *our* friend," Tiffany corrected her.

"Well she's closest to you. I told you, something about her doesn't sit right with me. Maybe it's because she always wants us to participate in her pity parties. Geesh, get over it and move on."

"You're so mean."

"No, I'm not. There just comes a time in a grown woman's life when you just have to put the past behind you and create something new. But anyway, enough about that crazy woman. I need you to sit down. I have something to tell you."

"What is it?"

"Sit down and take a sip of wine," Tommie ordered.

"You're starting to worry me," Tiffany said after taking a sip of wine.

"I found out who the Holy Roller Bandit is."

"You did? Who?"

Tommie looked at her friend for a few minutes before saying, "Lucien."

"Lucien who . . .?" Tiffany's mouth fell wide open. "Lucien Guillory? Your step-father Lucien? Our play father Lucien?"

Tommie nodded. "The one and only."

"Tommie this is not funny. What are you saying? The man that has killed all these women is the one and only Lucien Guillory? Get the heck out of here!"

"I'm afraid it's true," Tommie sighed. She told her friend how she found out Lucien was the HRB and how long he had been out of jail.

"Does his mother and father know about this?" Tiffany asked.

"Unfortunately, they're both dead. His father was murdered a few years back and his mother died a couple of years ago of cancer."

Tiffany was still in disbelief. "Tommie, do you think that Lucien is the one who has been trying to terrorize me?" Tiffany asked.

"Honestly, I don't know, but as I start to put the pieces together, I wouldn't rule it out."

"But why would he do this? And why me and not *you*?"

"I'm not one-hundred-percent sure, but I'm working over scenarios in my mind to figure out why he chose the women he chose." Tommie touched each of the photos that were laid out on the counter. "So far, the only thing I can come up with is that we were all at that conference. I still can't figure out why he would target the women from the conference. I still don't know how he knows about the conference or even who attended the conference. If my dates are correct Lucien was still in prison."

"I'm just in disbelief," Tiffany said pacing the kitchen floor. "Do you think we should cancel the girl's weekend?"

"Absolutely not. Like you said, we are not going to live in fear of this maniac. We're still going to have the girl's weekend and since you have all this space," Tommie said looking around the large home and giving hand gestures, "we're still going to have it here."

"Well okay then," Tiffany said, not sure of Tommie's idea.

"You're still packing right?"

"Three plus two!" Tiffany said with glee.

"Plus two?" Tommie asked.

"Yes ma'am. In addition to the three stooges, I also have Light 'Em Up and iStun."

"What?" Tommie said still confused. She watched her friend pull a flashlight from the utility drawer and walk to the couch to get her purse. When she returned she pulled out what looked like an iPhone. Tommie looked at her friend waiting for an explanation.

Tiffany showed Tommie the flashlight first. "This little puppy not only lights 'em up, but it *lights 'em up*! It's not just a flashlight, it's also a powerful stun gun. And this baby right here discharges three point five million volts of electricity," she said showing Tommie the fake iPhone.

"Get out of here. Where'd you get this stuff from?"

"One of my sponsors is a vendor for Divas in Action. You remember Sondra right?"

"Yes, I remember her. I like her."

"Well she is a sales rep for the company. They have tons of cute stuff for protection—especially for women. I ordered some other things, but they haven't arrived yet. And just so you know, this is what I'm getting all of you for Christmas."

"Christmas is never a surprise with you is it?"

"Says the re-gifter," Tiffany teased. Both the ladies laughed.

"I think we need to put the final touches on this girl's weekend. We only have a few days left," Tommie said.

"Let me text the girls and we can all get in on the conference line." Tiffany sent a group text to her girlfriends and dialed in from the phone in her office. She put the phone on speaker and waited for the other ladies to call in. As she waited, she noticed Tommie checking the windows and the exterior door.

"What's wrong?" she asked.

"Nothing," Tommie said. "Just making sure things are still secure. Looks good."

Almost all the ladies were on the call . . . except for Jillian. "Has anyone heard from Jillian with the exception of email?" Tiffany spoke into the speakerphone.

Everyone said no. "I was in Denver a few week ago," Kim said. "I call her and I tell her I would there and wanted to see her, but she never call me back, text or email."

"I had my sister go by her house a while back and she said that it looks like no one has been living there for a while, or at least no one has been home in a while. She says she's gone by there a few times. But I got the group text where she said she'd be at the girls weekend, so I wouldn't worry about it. We'll get her when she gets here."

"*If* she comes," Tommie mumbled.

The girls talked for over an hour making last minute plans for their weekend. Just as they were wrapping up their call, they all received a group text from Jillian saying she was confirming her attendance and her itinerary.

"Did you all just get that?" Tiffany asked.

"Umhmm," was all Tommie said. Something was going on with Jillian, and Tommie didn't like how it made her feel. She wondered if Jillian knew about Lucien's release.

Fifteen

Sunday, August 26, 2012

After navigating the church parking lot, Tommie ran inside to see if there was a decent seat left. She hated being late, but she had to stop by the precinct. Her captain wanted an update on the new information that had been obtained in the HRB case.

When Tommie arrived in the sanctuary, she could have sworn it was Easter or Christmas, because she saw ushers pulling chairs from the storage space for people to sit. She hated that, because someone always caught the Holy Ghost and either they would fall in her direction, or they'd trip over her feet.

She was relieved when she felt her cell phone vibrate. It was Tiffany.

Up front, on the left, second row.

Tommie went back and forth with the usher about where she was going to sit. She explained that someone was saving a seat for her, and the usher, who took her job much too seriously, continually tried to steer Tommie to the back, stating there were no more seats left up front.

"I *saaaiiid*, someone is saving a seat for me up front. Now, please remove your hands from me and go on about your business," Tommie said raising her voice. The usher gave her a '*hmph*', turned up her nose and continued ushering others to the extra seating.

"You're a lifesaver," Tommie told Tiffany once she made her way up front. She hugged her friend and said, "I almost had to put Mother Theresa in a head lock back there to get up here."

"Girl, I'm going to pray for you," Tiffany laughed.

"Please, because I need it. I almost felt the need to repent. She's lucky she took her hands off me."

Tiffany chuckled and shook her head at her friend. "What am I going to do with you?"

"Love and a whole lot of prayer. That should do the trick."

It took a while, but after moving from church to church, trying to find the right fit, she decided that this was the church for her. Pastor and First Lady Stowe had a teaching style that reached her and kept her interest. She had gone to churches where the preacher acted as if he was going into cardiac arrest after each sentence—total overkill. Then, there were those pastors she *knew* about—the ones that had women on the side, or those that had a drug dealer or two on their payroll, or even friends who ruffed those up that defied the pastor. Yes, being a police officer gave Tommie many advantages, and she knew she couldn't, with good conscious, sit in front of a preacher every Sunday, when she knew what he had done early that morning before the sermon, or whom he had done it to.

Tiffany had been coming to Destiny Christian Chapel for only a few months. She accepted Tommie's invitation one Sunday and had been coming every since.

"Did you know Fred Hammond was supposed to be here today?" Tiffany asked Tommie.

"No, I didn't, but that explains why there's standing room only. I don't know why I didn't know that."

"Because you've been buried in this case. It's understandable."

"I'll catch you up on the case after church is over."

The ladies and the entire congregation directed their attention to the praise and worship team, who began singing, *"Enter His Gates"* by Reverend Timothy Wright. Everyone began to sing along and the spirit was moving. They followed up with *"The Best in Me"* by Marvin Sapp, *"Thank You"* by Smokie Norful and concluded with *"I Smile"* by Kirk Franklin.

After the singing was done, First Lady Stowe stood at the microphone, gave all honor to God, and spoke of His goodness. She gave a few announcements and challenged the saints to be more like Him. After the first lady spoke, Deacon Burns lead the tithes and offering portion of the service.

"Can I borrow your pen?" Tommie asked Tiffany.

"Yes ma'am," she said handing her friend a designer ink pen. Both ladies made it a point to make their check out in the amount that was equal to ten percent of that weeks earning and then added an unselfish offering on top.

"I'm going to need you to start carrying a purse," Tiffany scolded her friend. "Your checkbook does not belong in your jacket pocket.

Tommie looked at her friend's patent leather Baguette Fendi purse. "No thank you," Tommie replied.

"I'm serious," Tiffany said.

"I am too. For how much that purse cost, I could pay my mortgage, car note, feed the hungry and still have enough to have an exotic vacation in Fiji."

"First of all, you don't have a mortgage payment. Your house is paid for and two, my purse did not cost that much. You don't have a clue how much it cost. I really got it for a steal."

"Well, I know it cost between two thousand and twenty five hundred, and if that's a steal, you were a victim."

Tiffany rolled her eyes and leaned over to her friend's ear. "Hater," she whispered. The two ladies directed their attention back to the pulpit with Pastor Stowe started preaching the word.

"Brothers and Sisters in Christ, uh, today, I want to talk to you about the company we keep. Now by a show of hands, how many of you watch the Real Housewives of Atlanta?"

Many of the young women in the congregation raised their hands and there was a loud chatter amongst them.

"Come on now. Now I know that some of you didn't raise your hand. You know you watch the housewives. I know, 'cause I see some of you talking about it on Facebook. But don't worry, I'm not here to tell you what you can and can't watch, but uh, I do believe that something in your spirit should cause you to change the channel."

The pastor received several hallelujahs and amens. Tommie could admit to watching the show a few times, but gave up on it after realizing how ignorant and crazy the women acted on the show. She was a professional and she couldn't have anyone associated her with the negativity of the show.

Tiffany saw enough comments on social media to make her never want to watch the show and she didn't.

"Ladies and gentlemen," the pastor continued, "reality television has gotten way out of hand. The sad part, besides the fact that some of you will watch it before coming to the house of the Lord, is, uh, that this is really reality. All of us *have*, *do* or *will* have some sort of drama in our lives. And, God knows we don't need to turn on the television to tune into someone else's drama."

The pastor paused for a moment. "A while ago, a couple came in from off the street and said that speaking with me was the last chance at saving their marriage. So, uh, I talked to this couple and the wife said that her husband could tell her everything that was going on with everyone else's life and relationship—both on and off television—but when it came to their relationship and discussing their problems, he didn't want to hear it. He was *sooo* busy worrying about everybody else's relationship that he couldn't see the problems in his own. And, when they were brought to his attention, he brushed them off, telling his wife, he didn't have a problem, so why should she. Or, or, he would roll his eyes, give a loud sigh or leave the room. Sometimes he would just leave the house. Little did he know that his wife was dying on the inside."

People in the congregation could be seen nodding or shaking their heads, while others made comments like, "my Lord", "yes", "you better preach pastor", or "help us Father."

"Yes, he was so enthralled in these reality shows and the relationships of his co-workers, that he didn't even realize that when he came home from work one evening, his wife had packed up her clothes and half of their belongings and moved out. He actually called her on her cell phone and asked her was she doing her usual spring cleaning and what was for dinner. Now, uh, I don't know about you folks, but something is deeply wrong when you come home and you can't tell that your wife has moved out of your house. It should be apparent that . . . that, Houston, we most definitely have a problem."

The pastor went on to preach about how the husband surrounded himself, or kept company with drama at work and on reality shows that he allowed them to consume him, and he lost his wife in the process. After the pastor was done with his sermon, the congregation stood up and gave a loud roar.

"Now, I know that I'm not really the reason some of you came today, so I'm going to get to the real reason you're here. Ladies and gentlemen, all the way from Dallas, Texas, the Dove Award winning, Stellar Award winning, Grammy Award winning, incomparable, Freeeeeeeeeeeeeed Hammond!"

The crowd went crazy, when Fred Hammond came out singing *"They That Wait."*

"Come on, put your hands together and sing it with me," the gospel singer shouted.

The congregation and the choir broke out in song.

"They that wait on the Lord, shall renew their strength. They shall mount up on wings, like an eagle in soar."

There was not a closed mouth in the entire church. After singing many of his number one hits, Fred Hammond left the pulpit and Pastor Stowe concluded the church service.

Tommie and Tiffany sat in their seats for a moment, allowing the crowd to thin as church was let out.

"I must admit, I do love me some Fred Hammond," Tiffany said.

"I do too," Tommie agreed. The two chatted about their favorite gospel music and which tunes stirred their spirits. Twenty minutes later, the crowd had thinned out and the two ladies deiced to head to Bone Fish Grill for an early dinner.

When they arrived at the restaurant, there was a thirty minute wait.

"We can stay here and wait, unless you have something else planned for tonight, then we can go somewhere else." Tiffany said.

Tommie gave the waitress her last name and took the guest pager. She and Tiffany opted to sit outside on one the patio benches, instead of the bar. "No, this is fine, because I want to talk to you about the case and I don't want to run the risk of anyone hearing me."

"So what's up?"

"I have this gut feeling that Jillian is up to something and something tells me that it has to do with this case," Tommie confided.

"What do you mean? Personally, I don't think she knows anything. I cannot imagine her knowing that Lucien has gotten out and not told any of us."

"Have you googled Lucien lately?"

"No. I should though."

"There are news articles, records and court records of his case all over the internet. And unless she never watches television, there is no way she can live right there and not know he was released."

"Hmm," Tiffany said. Tommie did have a point. Even if Jillian hadn't heard about it on the news, someone from the old neighborhood would have told her. "She has been acting very strange, withdrawn and suddenly she's too busy to call us."

"I'm telling you Tiff, I can't put my finger on it, but that girl is working with Lucien."

"I'm going to do the good Christian thing and give her the benefit of the doubt. I'm sure going to talk to her when she gets here. I think with all of us around her, she'll have no choice but to give us the truth or run, in which case we'll have our answer."

"Umhmm," was all Tommie said.

Sixteen

Tuesday, August 28, 2012

"Greensboro Police!" Tommie yelled with her standard Beretta issued hand gun drawn. She took a stance at the baseline of the front door of the forty-eight hundred square foot suburban home. Other police officers and a S.W.A.T. team also stood in various locations of the home—on the roof, on the side, at the back, with guns drawn, ready to take out their target.

"Greensboro Police!" Tommie yelled again. "Come out with your hands up!" she said slowly, careful to annunciate each word. "This is the last time I'm going to ask." Tommie waited a few seconds and gave hand gestures to the other offers to make their move.

"Cover me," she shouted and kicked in the front door to the Cape Cod Colonial. She ordered officers in various directions in the spacious home. Officers ran in every direction—upstairs, downstairs, bedrooms—in search of their suspect. The once manicured décor of the home was now a shambled mess as various officer's shouted, "Clear!"

When she was sure that every inch of the house was searched, Tommie met with leading officers at the large kitchen island.

"What do we have?" she asked as she took in her surroundings.

"No keys, purses or wallets," one said.

"Two cars in the garage," another said.

"We found fresh tracks disappearing into the woods outback. We have officers and dogs searching now," yet another said.

Tommie made her way out to the back deck and looked out into the wooded area. She observed that the nearest house on either side was at least three-hundred yards away. The wooded area out back donned at least one-hundred trees that disappeared into the night the further they went out. She looked around observing her surroundings, taking mental notes of every inch of the parameter.

"When you entered the house, was this door locked or unlocked?" she asked one of the command leaders.

"The French doors were unlocked detective," he answered her. Before he had even answered the question, Tommie already knew that their suspect had fled through the woods. Just as she was about to ask her next question, one of the officers called for her.

"Detective, I think you need to see this."

Tommy found her way into the study where the officer was. On the floor next to a cherry wood desk, was a bible. Just as she feared, she opened the bible and read the inscription, *'He without sin. ~~Judge'*.

The Holy Roller Bandit had struck again. Tommie had been working so hard to catch the culprit before another person was killed. She turned her attention back to the crime scene and requested that entire home be dusted for fingerprints.

"Something's not right here," she said to no one in particular. She drummed her fingertips on the top of the walnut desk. "What am I missing . . . what am I missing?" What looked like a drop of blood on the carpet next to the base of the desk caught her attention. She got down on her knees to investigate. Upon evaluating the spot, she was sure it was blood, only she didn't know how long it had been there, so it was hard to say if it was a fresh drop or not.

Her question was answered when saw a few more drops. The pattern was broken, but she was sure there was something to this splatter. After crawling around the desk, she saw it. A trail of blood from behind the desk seemed to disappear into the wall.

Tommie followed the trail and stopped at the wood paneled wall. She poked at the paneling. A home this elaborate had to have a revolving panel, a hidden safe. And, a study this prestigious had to have a hidden nook or cranny that held that safe. Personally, she kept her safe somewhere other than the obvious. But in her line of work, she found that many people with money were very much predictable. She observed the bookshelf behind the desk and mumbled to herself, “So predictable,” she mumbled.

“Excuse me detective?” one of the accompanying officers asked.

“There’s a secret compartment behind this bookshelf. Help me find it.” The officer looked at her puzzled.

“Trust me,” she told him. Together, they began poking around the paneled walls and book cases, searching behind books and portraits, which in Tommie’s opinion, were some of the ugliest she’d ever seen. She got on the floor and tried to follow the trail of blood on the floor. She pressed on the shelf right where it disappeared.

“Bingo!” the shelf clicked and came ajar. Tommie pulled the panel completely opened and her hopes of finding Evangelist Mary Roberts alive faded. The famous evangelist and her husband were tied together, in just their underwear in the secret panic room. Mr. Roberts had been shot in his temple, while Mrs. Roberts was shot center mass in the chest.

Tommy lowered her head and said a silent prayer for the couple. The Roberts were the sixth and seventh victim of the Holy Roller Bandit. Mr. Roberts was his first spousal casualty. Tommie had not put her finger on the Holy Roller Bandit’s cause, but she was sure of one thing—he was looking for revenge.

She read the inscription in the bible to herself repeatedly. She couldn’t figure it out. What connection did he have with these people? She thought back to the other cases and tried to pin point what they all had in common. Besides the fact that Mrs. Roberts and the others were either evangelists or high profile pastor wives, the only other thing they had in common . . . was . . . her. She had to been to each of the churches in which the deceased had gained their fame and they all had attended the women's conference. She pulled out her cell phone and dialed.

"Hi Lacy, it's Tommie . . . I'm doing fine, I hope you're doing well . . . Yes . . . Yes . . . Well, I wanted to know if you remembered the Ladies Choice Conference we went to a last year . . Yes, that one . . . Off the top of your head, can you remember who all was there?" Tommie nodded her head as Lacy spoke, giving an occasional, "Umhmm . . . Umhmm . . . Umhmm."

Lacy, one of the church administrators, had confirmed Tommie's fear. All the women who had been killed were in attendance at that conference. She spoke into her cell phone.

"Compile list of all attendees at that conference." If she wasn't too sure before that the women's conference had a connection, she was one-hundred-percent positive now. She finally had a valuable lead in the case. She didn't know where the HRB would strike next, but she could warn the survivors who had attended that conference.

She stopped for a moment, when she remembered that Tiffany reminded her that all of her girlfriends were at that conference as well. She was about to dial Tiffany's number, when an officer interrupted her.

"Detective," one of the officers said as he entered the study. "You may want to come upstairs. We found two children."

Tommie gasped.

"They're okay. A little shaken, but they're okay. They were locked in one of the bedrooms upstairs."

Tommy followed the officers up the spiral staircase to what she assumed was the master suite. The children were locked in what looked like another panic room. This one was larger than that last.

When the little blond-haired, blue-eyed girl saw Tommie, she immediately ran into her arms. She had to be at least six-years-old. She hadn't responded to any of the big bad officers with the scary guns, but she immediately felt drawn to Tommie. She was in a pair of shorts and a Sponge Bob Square Pants t-shirt, but had on no shoes. Her face was wet and dirty—Tommie was sure from crying.

Her brother, on the other hand, wasn't so welcoming. In fact, he seemed to be in a state of shock. He lay belly down under a storage cabinet. His pale white skin had wet and dry tear stains on it like his sister. For a moment, Tommie didn't think the young lad was breathing until she saw him blink his eyes. He had to be younger than his sister.

"Hi handsome, I'm detective . . . police officer Tommie. Can you come from under there for me?" Tommie held the little girl while she reached her hand out to the boy, but he did not move.

"What's your name?" Tommie asked the little girl.

"Laura," she said.

"What's his name," she asked nodding towards the frightened little boy.

"His name is Lucas," the little girl answered.

"Lucas, can you come out so I can make sure you're okay. You can trust me."

"He won't trust anybody. That's what the bad man said to my Mommy. "

"What else did the bad man say to your mommy?"

"He told her to trust him and tell him where daddy was. She did tell him, but the bad man hurt daddy."

"Is that all?"

"Yes. Um. I think. When the bad man went to look for Daddy, Mommy hid us in here. She told us not to move until she came back. Is it okay to come out now?"

"Mommy!" Lucas let out a screeching scream.

Seventeen

"Dammit!" Tommie said as she hit the hood of her police issued SUV. She was upset that she had to release those two innocent children to child protective services until they could locate the next of kin for the Roberts. They had lost both their parents at once and what they had witnessed would have a lasting effect on them for the rest of their lives. They would need years of counseling, especially Lucas. She took in a deep breath and let it out.

She leaned against the truck and scanned her surroundings. She could feel him. He was still here, watching, but she was unsure where. He could be in the woods, or he could be in one of the nearby homes. She decided not to launch a full search of each home as she was sure it would set off Lucien and cause him to kill yet another innocent victim.

"I know you can see me you bastard," she said into the chilly air. She knew wherever he was, he could tell what she was saying. "I'm going to get you, and when I do, they are going to fry you like they should have done the first time. Your days are numbered. It's only a matter of time before I check your clock. You can count on that." With those words, Tommie got into her vehicle and headed back to the station.

She thought back to the beginning. The precinct had received an anonymous call from someone who claimed that they saw a strange man break into the Roberts' home, but there were no signs of forced entry at the home. Lucien was playing with her and she was going to play with him. But like her Chess game, she was going to stay one step ahead of him, and when she was done . . . checkmate.

*****

Tommie had been right. Lucien had been watching her. He had a close call. He couldn't figure out how the detective could have known he'd be there. He had heard the sirens from at least a mile away before running out into the woods and to the busy highway behind them. Paige was waiting for him.

They stayed and watched for a moment until the police dogs caught on to his scent and took off into the woods. He instructed Paige to drive down the busy highway and get off at the next exit. They drove until they found themselves in the same position in the woods behind the house. The dogs had been called off, but through his binoculars, Lucien could see half of the Greensboro Police Department in and around the parameter of the house.

He saw Tommie leaning against her SUV in the grassy area on the side of the home. He had read her lips loud and clear. How dare she think she was better than he was. He had to take care of a few more people, and then he was coming for her. She would pay like just like the others.

*****

Back at the station, Tommie saw Detective Sykes sitting at his desk. "I thought you would have stayed back at the crime scene," Tommie said walking up behind him.

The detective nearly jumped out of his skin. He quickly closed his browser and said, "Yeah, well, I needed to get back here to see if I could put some of the pieces together."

"Did you come up with anything?" she asked walking to the coffee station and filling her large coffee mug.

"Not yet. I'm still trying to figure out why Lucien is here in the Triad. Denver, I can understand and Atlanta, I can understand. But why here? You're the only connection he has here and yet he hasn't come after you."

Tommie wanted to share her new theory with John, but didn't want to feed him too much information. She was a very observant person and had noticed the changes that John had made since the beginning of this case. Now, he was jumpy and nervous. She didn't know what it was, but something wasn't right about him. Right now, she didn't have the time to figure it out, she had to find Lucien and make sure he was prosecuted to the fullest extent of the law. But what she did tell him surprised him.

"Well, I can't figure out the connection either, except the fact that I knew every last one of those deceased women."

"I need to go to the hole," John said all of a sudden, securing his cell phone on his belt. "I'll be back in a minute," he told his partner.

Tommie pretended not to be paying attention, but she was. Although her back was facing him, she could see his reflection through the crime board. John seemed nervous and fidgety as he looked back at her to make sure she was not watching him. But she was—she was watching him real closely.

When her partner was out of her sight, she dialed Tiffany's number.

"Hey darling, how are you?"

"Good," Tiffany said. "How are you? I saw on the news that that creep has struck again."

"You don't know the half of it. Are you about ready for the girl's arrival?"

"Yes ma'am, but I know that's not why you called me. What's up?"

Tiffany knew Tommie well. It was one of the reasons that out of all of the girls, she and Tiffany were the closest. She trusted her friend with her life and in turn, Tiffany trusted Tommie with hers.

"Listen, do you still have your private investigator connections?"

"On speed dial," Tiffany responded. Tiffany was a valuable asset. Like her best friend, she had people in high and low places, and together they pooled their resources together . . . making them a dangerous pair. Those resources came in handy when Tiffany needed to tie up the final details that won her that hefty divorce settlement.

"I need a favor . . ." she said and gave Tiffany all the details. Once they were done, Tiffany asked Tommie if she'd be staying with her that night or at her own place.

"Well you've got three plus two," she chuckled at that thought. "But if you want me to come and stay with you, I'd be happy to, or if you want a change of scenery, you can come to may place."

"Give me a few hours," Tiffany said. "Then I'll call you with my answer. I've got so much to do around here and I know you've got your hands full there."

"This is true. Talk to you later," Tommie said. This time Tiffany beat Tommie and ended the call first.

Tommie was done with her call when John returned from the bathroom.

"Wow, did you blow it out? You were gone an awfully long time. You know, I've heard horror stories about the men's john."

John gave a nervous laugh. "Well, uh, I, umm, yes it must have been my lunch. I don't think it's agreeing with me."

Tommie knew John was lying, what she didn't know was why. "What did you have for lunch? And you went without me? Awww man, you didn't even bring me anything back," she teased.

"Well, umm, you were so busy and what I had for lunch wasn't the least bit healthy," he tried to explain.

"I'm just joking with you John," Tommie said, finally letting him off the hook. This could go on forever and she didn't have time for it.

John sat his cell phone on his desk and went to the coffee station to fill up his cup. Tommie watched him suspiciously. When he turned around, he noticed that his partner was staring at him.

"What?" he asked, taken aback.

"You know, I was thinking, Lucien killed the Roberts but he didn't harm the children."

"He, umm, probably didn't know they were there."

"He knew they were there, trust me. But I wonder if he was trying to send a message, or is he just getting sloppier."

Before Detective Sykes made the anonymous call to the police station, Lucien had told him he would not harm the children. John had told him he would be making a mistake by leaving the children behind. And although they hadn't said much, the Roberts girl had said enough to cause Tommie to expect something.

"I don't know. I'll tell you one thing," he said, "this entire case is taking its toll on me."

Tommie walked over to the crime board. It wasn't that she didn't hear what her friend had said, but she had to find a killer. "So," she said, tracing facts on the board, "Lucien Guillory is released from the Colorado Department of Corrections eight months ago. Two months ago, women of faith start dropping like flies. At each crime scene, he leaves a bible with the inscription, *'He without sin.' ~~Judge.* Those bibles were purchased with a prepaid debit card purchased at a Denver drug store and purchased by a one Paige Guillory." Tommie was silent. So was her partner. She could tell his thoughts were a million miles away.

"So we know that Lucien has one or more accomplices and his strategy spans at least three states. We know that between the deaths of both his parents, he received two insurance policies and a trust fund that totaled millions of dollars."

That caught John's attention. "Millions? I don't understand."

"Well, when Lucien's father died years ago, he left a hefty insurance policy behind along with a few investments and other assets. It would appear that Lucien's mother put half of what she received from her late husband's assets into accounts for Lucien, provided he ever got out of prison. If he did not get out, the accounts would default to any off spring he may have fathered." Tommie didn't look directly at John, but she was a master at peripheral vision. John had turned redder than a beet.

"And then, when his mother passed away, she left him everything she had with instruction that if Lucien never saw the outside of a jail cell, the assets would default to his children or other grandchildren—in that order."

John was now beginning to sweat. Lucien never mentioned to him the millions he had stored up. Lucien had told him that his mother had left a small insurance policy and he would split it with him if he helped him with his plan.

"How did you find all of this information," John inquired.

"Oh, I have my sources," Tommie answered.

"I have to get home now. The Mrs. Has been nagging that I don't spend quality time with her and the kiddos. Yanno, gotta try to find time to fulfill my husbandly and fatherly duties," he said. "I'll talk to you tomorrow. Go home and get some rest TL." With that, John disappeared from the police station.

Tommie sat in her chair, kicked her feet up and crossed them across her desk. *I think I found a mole*, she thought to herself. Not only was she going to bring Lucien to justice, but she'd make sure John was there right along with him.

Eighteen

Lucien hid in a storage closet in the house at 27 Flagship Cove. He was quiet for a long while. He had to make sure Tiffany was not home. He had gone this long undetected, he wasn't about to ruin things now. When he didn't hear any movement upstairs, he carefully made his way up the basement stairs. When he got to the main level, he stopped for a moment and observed his surroundings. He was sure that Tiffany wasn't home when he saw that the alarm system was set to away. He knew that she had ADT revamp her security system, but had caught her at a moment of vulnerability.

He was in the back of the house, when he heard the garage door open. She had disarmed the alarm but was distracted when one of her neighbors, who was driving through the neighborhood, stopped to chat with her. Tiffany had left the door open and Lucien had snuck in and cut the wires that were connected to the basement door and its windows.

Lucien froze when the phone rang. The call went to voice mail. It was Tommie.

"Hey beautiful, looks like you might be on your way here, so I'll try you on your cell." Lucien let out a sigh of relief and went into the kitchen to see what was available to eat. He looked throughout Tiffany's fridge, frowning at his choices. Although Tiffany loved fine dining, she kept nothing but healthy foods in her home, if she kept anything at all. He frowned at the tofu, protein shakes, vegetables, flax seed and other healthy items she had. He was hard pressed to find anything that had regular packaging, like Harris Teeter or Food

Lion. Instead, her food had come from Trader Joes, Earth Fare and Whole Foods.

The vibrating phone on his hip caught his attention. It was Paige. The text read: *Your chance is coming sooner than you know. This weekend.*

Lucien wanted to make Tommie and her girlfriends pay for sending him to prison. That included Paige. Lucien was starting to become a little concerned when he realized that Paige was becoming a bit distant. The truth was, Paige was having a hard time keeping her life with Lucien separated from what she called her real life. She didn't need added complications trying to explain it to her girlfriends. A liar and deceiver can only keep up a facade for so long, but when you add extras into the mix, things really begin to unravel.

Now Lucien would get his chance. How lucky could he be? All of them would be in the same place and he could kill them all at once. He'd kill his main suspect—Tommie, and her friends—including Paige. He'd have no use for her. She would have served her purpose.

Lucien had escaped suspicion in Denver, where his two former attorneys were found executed. The cops that beat him half to death were involved in an unexplained accident and the cop who was responsible for Lucien's release was found hanging from the gable in his attic. The suicide note that Lucien had left was realistic enough for an open and shut case.

Out of the twelve jurors, Lucien, with the help of Paige's cyber stalking skills, could only locate four. The families were still searching for three of them. One of the bodies was found floating in Sloan's Lake, nearly three months after their disappearance.

Lucien made sure he was always available if the Aurora Police Department came knocking with questions. He used Paige's condo as his address of residence. He had looked up one of his old buddies who owned a garage when he was released from prison. Lucien would show up occasionally and used it as his place of employment. Although he didn't need it, Lucien would accept a check from his buddy, cash it and turn around give it back to him. The ten dollars an hour was nothing compared to the millions Lucien's mother had stored up for him. With all these things in place, any suspicion was soon erased.

According to the Colorado Department of Corrections, Lucien was an upstanding citizen after being released, after fifteen years in prison. However, they did not forget the fact that he had killed a woman, and for that, Lucien could never own a firearm, he had to attend anger management and rehabilitation classes and he had to check in with a parole officer at least once a week, until the courts felt he was one-hundred-percent rehabilitated.

He knew he was being watched, so he had to be careful. He also knew Paige was being watched and because of that, he didn't completely trust her. He had learned years ago to never trust women. The only woman he did trust was his mother, and now she was gone.

Lucien sent a text back to Paige that read: *Gracias!* He proceeded to try to find something edible in Tiffany's fridge, but his quest was interrupted when he heard the alarm system beep. It has been disarmed. Tiffany was supposed to be at Tommie's. He heard a key in the lock as he quickly looked around in an effort to find an escape route. He didn't have too many choices, so he quickly closed himself in the large kitchen pantry. He hoped she had just forgotten something and had planned on leaving again. If not, if she opened the door, he'd just have to kill her.

He heard Tiffany walk into the kitchen and open the fridge. He looked around to see what he could use to render his victim unconscious before he would killed her. He was relieved when he heard her talking.

"Hey Tommie, sorry I'm running late. I had to stop by home to get the paperwork I was talking to you about. I think it would be great if the Greensboro PD could be one of our sponsors. I'm so excited how this project is turning out." Tiffany took a gulp of the bottled water she had retrieved from fridge.

"You're not drinking already are you," Tommie asked her friend.

"No, I was thirsty. I'm drinking water. I'm on my way. Talk to you in a bit," she said to her friend before ending the call. With that, Tiffany had disappeared into the garage and armed the alarm system. Lucien stood by the laundry door, listened as Tiffany backed her truck out of the garage, and let the garage door down.

That was close, Lucien thought to himself. He wasn't prepared, but he knew what to do if and when necessary. This time he thought against raiding Tiffany's fridge and sent Paige another message:

Pick me up in 10. I'm not staying.

He exited the home from the basement. He had disabled the motion censored light and she slid off into the darkness. Paige was waiting for him two blocks over.

"What happened?" Paige asked once he was in the car. Paige had plans and was irritated that Lucien had disturbed them. She and a friend were supposed to spend some time at her home in Denver. The one she thought Lucien knew nothing about—but he did. It was amazing how many eyes one could have when money was involved. There was nothing that Paige did that Lucien did not know about. Now he eyed her in the car, wishing he could reveal to her that he knew the reason behind her irritability.

"What's up with you?" he asked.

"Nothing. I was just about to wash my hair when you called. Is everything okay?"

"Yes. Everything is copasetic."

"What does that mean," Paige asked. For a white woman that had grown up in a predominately upper middle class African American neighborhood, Paige acted pretty dumb.

"It means that everything is alright. You know, okie dokie?" he smiled at his insult. Paige didn't think it was too funny. He had ruined her night with Anthony. She'd called him right after Lucien had texted her to let him know something had come up and she had to take a rain check.

"So what happened?" Paige asked.

"Your girl came back for a brief moment. But I thought hard after you sent that text. If I had taken her out tonight, that would have raised too much suspicion. Since you said you all will be together this weekend, I figured I'd just wait until then and get them all at the same time." Lucien turned to Paige and held her chin. "This is why I need you to be on your a-game baby. I'm going to need you to make sure this all happens without any interruptions. Everything needs to be in place. And, once this is all over, you and I can live happily ever after."

Paige gave Lucien one of her fake smiles. She may have been crazy, but she wasn't completely stupid. She knew that once Lucien finished his crime spree, he would have no choice but to kill her. She knew way too much. He thought she was stupid and she liked it that way. He would never know that she was preparing her escape.

Paige knew Lucien's mother had died and had even attended the funeral. She knew there was no way Lucien would know because any family he had left had disowned him. Lucien's two sisters and half brother swore they'd never forgive Lucien for what he had done. They knew he had stabbed Tommie's mother to death and because of it, *their* mother's health had suffered. She always worried that someone would kill Lucien in prison.

For some reason, out of all her children, Lucien was her favorite. Perhaps it was because he was her first born. Once their father had died, Lucien's siblings tried to keep their mother from having any contact with Lucien, but she wrote him on occasion. She informed him that if he beat this case, there was money waiting for him to get back on his feet and then more. What Lucien didn't know was that

Paige had stock piled a lot of his money. At his mother's funeral, Lucien's sisters had given Paige several letters than were never mailed. They were unopened. The sisters asked that Paige nor Lucien ever contact the family again.

Paige had read the letters from Lucien's mother. Her mouth fell wide open when she read one that detailed accounts that she had set up for her son should he be released from prison—complete with account numbers, debit cards, online banking passwords and everything Paige needed to access the accounts. Working in IT, she easily hacked other accounts, after all, Lucien didn't know about them, so the incidents went undisputed and unnoticed.

Nineteen

Wednesday, August 29, 2012

Tommie walked into the precinct bright and early. She and Tiffany had a productive meeting the night before. She was able to help Tiffany finalize the plans for the entrepreneurial conference and Tiffany was able to help her get the goods she needed to get on her partner. She took the information she had detailed from the day she suspected John's involvement with the Holy Roller Bandit to the Captain.

"You do realize we have to have a reasonable cause before we go accusing one of our own don't you? I already think you're too close to this case." Captain Randall had said once Tommie presented her suspicions.

"Yes sir. I know," Tommie responded. "That's why I waited a few weeks before saying anything." Tommie laid out all the information she had on Detective John Sykes. Tiffany's private detective connection had gotten everything there was to get on her partner, right down to the large deposit into a secret checking account.

"And just why are you investigating Sykes on your own. It's almost as if there is some personal tie here. Am I missing something TL?" Captain Randall had suspected John for some time. He just didn't know for what. He, too, had noticed the detectives odd behavior and he knew that since Tommie worked close with the detective, she knew more. She was one of his best, if not *the* best, detectives the department had.

"Yes sir. I have reason to believe that the HRB is targeting my friends—and me." Tommie let that set in for a moment. She hadn't thought about it until now.

"What makes you think this?" the captain asked. Tommie had to tread lightly. If she was going to accuse one of their own, she darn well better be right.

"Sir, besides all that you see there, in our investigation, we struggled for a while to figure out what all the victims of this case had in common."

The captain leaned back in his leather chair, glasses barely hanging onto his nose.

"Sir, every last one of those women attended a conference a while back. In addition, I was there, and so were all of my friends."

"I'm still not understanding," the chief interjected.

"Then, I found out someone has been stalking my friend Tiffany," she said.

"The one that bought that big house in her divorce settlement?"

"Yes that one. She contacted me after she started feeling as if someone was watching her. I inspected her house and sure enough, there are signs of breaking and entering, like broken locks. And, if that wasn't strange enough, there things left in her attic as if someone was living there." She paused to see if the captain was still with her. When he nodded, she continued.

"John started acting strange when I started giving him details of the case. When I would give him a bit of pertinent information, he would disappear and say he had to go make a phone call or go to the hole. Whenever I walk by his desk he jumps, shuts down windows on his pc. And when I was telling him that my connection to this case, you'd thought he would have seen a ghost. He then left to make a phone call. Well, this has been going on for a while." Tommie tried to recount as many incidents she could with the detective. "It's almost as if he's one step ahead of me. When I show up to a crime scene, he's already there. When I make a bee-line to the precinct, and I've left before him, he's always beat me back."

"I can see where that might be suspicious," the captain said, leaning forward on his desk. He closed both hands close to his mouth as if he was in great thought.

"This is why I had one of my connections check him out." She did not want to reveal Tiffany as her source. If the case ever went to court, Tiffany could be prosecuted and she could be charged. "First we checked his phone records and there are several calls going to a (303)555-5622 and (303)555-7981."

"Those are Colorado area codes," the chief said.

"Right, and guess who one of those numbers is registered to?"

"Who?"

"A Paige Guillory."

"The HRB is married?"

"We couldn't find any records confirming that. We didn't find any records on a Paige Guillory . . . *period.* There were a couple of other numbers in the report that had the 303 area code, but they turned out to be burn phones. Another one had a 404 area code, that's where the HRB is from. And then there's this 336 number," she said pointing to the number on the file. "We also found a large deposit going into this secret account. I'm telling you Captain, he's involved somehow."

The sergeant listened to the rest of Tommie's story before saying. "Okay. We'll keep him under strict surveillance, but you can't let him know what we suspect. You need to be careful, because if he is involved, there is no telling what he'll do. We don't need any more loss of life, and I certainly don't want to lose my best detective."

Tommie agreed and now that the captain was aware, more eyes were on Detective John Sykes.

When Tommie exited the sergeant's office, Detective Sykes was at his computer. Just like clockwork, he clicked his computer as Tommie got nearer.

"What was that about?" he asked Tommie, nodding towards the captain's office.

"I told you about the conference Tiffany is putting on right?" John nodded. "Well she's trying to get a shoe in to see if she can get the GSO PD to become a sponsor. I think it's a good idea. The GSO PD working hand in hand with local entrepreneurs. If we can work it, we'll have a recruitment booth at the conference, and maybe get some new recruits in to help us with the backlog." One of the things that made her a good detective was that Tommie knew how to think on her feet.

"You have to be one step ahead of everyone else," her father had told her. In fact, he had taught her everything she knew.

"Yeah, I hope that works out for you," was all he said.

"Well you're on your own this weekend. But you know how to reach me. And John," she stopped.

"What?"

"Only call me if it is an emergency. I haven't spent a weekend with the girls in a while. I really need this. I want this guy as much as you do, but I'm not going to let this disrupt my life."

"So, are you ladies convening at your place or Tiffany's?" the detective inquired.

"You have to ask?" Tommie said, playfully laughing at her partner.

"Uh, yeah, I guess you're right. Hey, I gotta go to the hole, but you have fun, and I promise not to call you unless it's an emergency."

Tommie smiled and watched her partner walk towards the precinct exit—opposite of the hole. Tommie turned around and looked towards her boss's office. The captain had witnessed the scene that had just transpired. He nodded towards Tommie, she nodded back.

Tommie dialed Tiffany's number.

"Hello," Tiffany answered.

"Hey beautiful, are you ready for the weekend?"

"I am so ready!" her friend shouted. "How about you?"

"I can't wait. Hey, I talked to the chief. He still has to get final approval, but we can have a recruitment booth at the conference. God knows we need the help around here. But, I can't guarantee the dollar amount. That's between *his* people and *your* people."

"That's okay. I understand, and I thank you for helping me with this. Even if they don't donate a whole lot, their presence will give me mucho brownie points. Did I tell you that you sold the most tickets?"

Tiffany had challenged her friends, telling them she'd give one-thousand dollars of her own money to whichever of her girlfriends could sell the most tickets. The other ladies felt they were at a disadvantage. Between Tommie's location, connections at the precinct, her church and her book club, she was able to sell seventy-five tickets.

"You can keep that money. Save it and put in a trust account for my future niece and nephew," Tommie said clearing her throat, hinting that Tiffany needed to have children, because *she* hadn't planned on having any.

"You definitely need a vacation because you've lost your mind if you think I'm going to let a child distort this beautiful body," Tiffany said.

Tommie rolled her eyes. "You're going to deny me a niece and nephew to spoil?"

"I'll tell you what," Tiffany said. "You have children and I'll help you spoil them." Both the ladies laughed.

"You know we're sad, don't you?" Tommie asked her good friend.

"Yes ma'am. Let's go buy ourselves a dog," Tiffany suggested.

"Ha-ha. That's about as close as I'm going to get to a child," Tommie responded.

After the two ladies talked for a few more moment, Detective Sykes walked back into the precinct.

"I've got to go, but I will see you all tomorrow," Tommie told Tiffany. "Do you have the flight information for the girls?"

"Yes," Tiffany answered. "But I am going to be speaking at Bennett College tomorrow—last minute. But I will still have time to pick up the girls from the airport."

"Okay. Just in case, email me the information. I'll be stopping by dad's grave before I come. I'll see you tomorrow." The two ladies exchanged *"I love yous"* and ended the call.

"Oh hey John. I didn't expect to see you before I left. Is everything alright?" Tommie said directing her attention to her partner.

"Oh, uh, everything is fine. You girls have fun. And if I don't get a chance to tell you, Happy Birthday."

"Awww that's so sweet of you," Tommie said, hugging her partner. It took everything in her power to do so. "Aren't you forgetting something?"

"What?" the detective asked her.

Tommie held out her hand. "Stop playing John. Out with it, now."

The detective's face turned beet red. Tommie was enjoying toying with the scoundrel. "What?" he asked again.

"Where is my gift man?" she shouted.

The detective let out a sigh of relief and said, "I don't even give my wife birthday gifts. If I gave you one, people would begin to talk. You know, think something was going on between you and me." The detective had grown quite cocky.

"And we both know that would never happen right?" Tommie asked. She waited to see the deflated look on the deflated detective's face before gathering her coat and her bag from her desk. When she looked back at the detective, he had a scowl on his face.

Tommie smiled at her partner and patted his shoulder on her way out of the precinct. The detective mumbled something to himself and didn't know that Captain Randall was watching him. As soon as Tommie was out of sight, the detective dialed Lucien's number.

Twenty

Thursday, August 30, 2012

Tiffany took time from her foundation and projects to prepare for her girlfriend's visit. She had to speak before a group of young ladies at Bennett College in a few hours. It was one of the historically black colleges in North Carolina. Her topic was entrepreneurship and an anonymous donor had donated funds for fifty seniors to attend the conference.

Tiffany was excited about seeing her girlfriends again. After all that had been going on, she welcomed the company and the distraction.

She could have hired a housekeeper or cleaning service to clean her home, but she had always said if a place was too big to clean, it was too big to live in. And although her home stayed immaculate, she could only guess how thick the dust buildup was on her furniture. There were parts of her house she had rarely even visited and she could hear Tommie's voice in her head. *Who buys a house this big anyway? That's just crazy!* She knew Tommie was right, but she wouldn't admit it to her. She knew she didn't buy the house to prove anything to Richard or anyone else. She had bought the house just because she could. She had envisioned a place for all her girlfriends and a place to hold elaborate parties and functions. The thought of selling the large home had crossed her mind, but she soon killed that though.

She put on a pair of yellow rubber gloves and retrieved her cleaning cart from the laundry room. The rolling cart was complete with feather dusters, rags, cleaning chemicals, fresheners and everything she needed to clean her home.

Tiffany went from room to room, space to space cleaning every inch of her home. She dusted, waxed wood, dusted and mopped floors, cleaned toilets, sinks and tubs. She kept a supply of Bath and Body Works Fresh Bamboo Wallflowers and made sure there was one in most of the homes electrical sockets. On her last trip, the young sales representative asked her if she owned a business. Tiffany had bought two-hundred of the wallflowers along with an equal amount of bacterial hand soap. When Tiffany told her yes, the young lady gave Tiffany a card and contact information for one of their distribution managers. She advised that since she bought these items in bulk and on a regular basis, she could probably get them at a discount. And, even though Tiffany didn't need a discount, she was frugal when she wanted to be and she was going to take advantage of that discount. Not only did she use them at home, she used them at the office, gave them to her employees and her friends and occasionally included them in gift baskets.

Tiffany was amazed that she was able to clean every inch of the house in record time. She felt she had just the right amount of space for each of her friends to have their own room and on-suite. Each of the rooms had a touch of personalization for each woman. They would always tease her that once she got a husband, they'd no longer be able to stay with her and her new husband would convert the rooms, stripping them of all their memories. Truth be told, the last thing Tiffany was thinking about was a husband. She had been there and done that, although she didn't mind having a play date every now and then.

"If I do ever get married again, which I doubt, you all could still stay here. You could occupy the left wing and he'd never even know you were here." She had a point. She was sure of one thing. If she ever got married again, there would have to be an understanding—he would have to have his own home because he couldn't move into hers and he could only stay overnight on the weekends . . . you know, for conjugals.

Tiffany looked at the time on her Cartier watch. She had a little time to get ready and get to Bennett College to give her motivational speech. The event would only take an hour and from there she would head to the airport to pick up her friends.

*****

After speaking to the lovely women at Bennett College, Tiffany felt good about her efforts. She was always happy to see young women of color striving for success. It was refreshing to be able to see that the world of the black woman didn't consist of living beyond their means, trying to impress people they didn't like or who didn't like them, and fighting and acting a plain plum fool on television. She had attended a think tank with a cultural group, made of a mostly non-African American panel on "Views and Distinction of the Black Woman." Some of the things she heard and learned sickened her. She made sure she didn't leave the meeting without making it very clear that all black women aren't what you see on television and that something had to be done about that stereotype.

She took photos with the college students and answered a few more questions before heading off to the airport.

Jillian and Kim's plane landed at PTI Airport within minutes of each other. Tiffany was waiting for them curbside.

"This is crazy," Jillian said as she helped Tiffany put her luggage into the back of her Range Rover.

"What is?" Tiffany asked her.

"I could have flown into Charlotte for a hundred dollars less," she complained. In no way could her friends know that she had actually had Lucien drop her off at the airport with her luggage and that she hadn't actually flown into Greensboro. They couldn't know she had been here for days.

"Yes, and you could have rented a car and drove an hour and a half from Charlotte to Greensboro . . . and it's nice to see you too!"

"I'm sorry," Jillian said hugging her friend. Tiffany could tell that Jillian had a lot on her mind and made a mental note to ask her about it once they were alone. Although the women held no secrets and could talk openly in front of each other, Tiffany was usually a good judge of character and knew this was not the time to ask Jillian about what was bothering her.

"I tell you, you get more beautiful every time I see you," Kim told Jillian as she gave her a hug.

"Me?" Jillian exclaimed. "Look at you, my exotic queen."

"And look at you Tiffany. Divorce definitely looks good on you Mami." The three ladies shared a laugh.

"Where's Maria?" Jillian asked Tiffany.

"She should be in a little later on. Unlike you, she did fly into Charlotte," Tiffany said snidely.

As the ladies drove from the airport, Jillian and Kim played the "brake game." They always said Tiffany drove like a mad woman and scared them so bad that they often found themselves pumping their imaginary breaks.

Tiffany could sense Kim, who sat in the front seat, playing the game and she couldn't help but laugh. "I know you're not acting like you are scared of my driving, you live in California."

"True, but they no drive like this in San Diego."

"But you're always in L.A and I know *they* drive crazy there."

Tiffany noticed that Jillian was mighty quiet. She looked at her through her rear view mirror. Jillian was looking out the window and had a faraway look on her face.

"You okay back there?" she asked.

"I'm good," Jillian said without looking up. Tiffany reminded herself that Tommie expressed to her that Jillian was somehow involved with Lucien. She made a note to mention Jillian's odd behavior to Tommie.

"When you decide to go red," Kim asked her. "I like a that look on you."

"Thank you. Just a few months ago. Trying to do something new. I like it most days, but others, it's a monster to contend with . . . you know, the roots and all," Jillian answered finally looking away from the window.

"I like it," Kim reiterated.

"I like it too," Tiffany said. "I'm going to see if Nairobi has that color for black hair."

"Nairobi?" Kim asked.

"Yes. That's what my beautician uses to perm my hair. Not all of us can have naturally straight hair."

"But you mixed," Kim exclaimed.

"True, but I was awarded hair from my father's side of the family."

The women continued to chatter about their various uses of hair products and recommendations on what worked and what didn't.

Tiffany's cell phone rang and she answered it via her SUV's dashboard.

"Hey Maria."

"Hey Diva, where are you guys?"

"On our way home. Where are you?"

"At your place," she said.

"I thought you were getting in later. And how did you get in? I had the locks changed."

"I was but I decided to catch an earlier flight. And I stopped by the station and got the key from Tommie. Now, hurry up and get her because I'm hungry and as usual you haven't cooked anything."

Tiffany thought that was odd. Tommie had told her she was taking the day off. "Tommie's at work?" Tiffany asked her.

"Yeah she said she got a break in that case she's been working on. She said she shouldn't be long."

Tiffany noticed Jillian's reaction to Maria's revelation. Jillian, who just moments ago, was lost in thought, sat up straight and looked towards the dashboard of the SUV.

"Okay," Tiffany said. She was curious now. "Make yourself at home. You know where the fridge and the food is. It's not like there isn't food. Tommie bought groceries a couple of days ago."

"Tofu? Food? Humph!" was Maria's response.

"Don't knock it until you try it," Tiffany said. "But I know there's other food in there."

"Just hurry up and get here. I want us all here before Tommie gets here." Maria laughed and disconnected the call .

"That girl is crazy," Jillian said. "You know she's going to eat you out of house and home."

"She sure is," Kim cosigned.

Twenty-One

Tiffany pulled up to her security gate. "Something look different," Kim said.

"Someone bought that plot over there and built that house."

"A bit too much if you ask me," Jillian mumbled from the backseat.

"What?" Tiffany asked her.

"I think is a bit too much for one person," Jillian clarified. If Jillian was looking to put a gray cloud over this girl's weekend, she was sadly mistaken.

"You could be right. Perhaps if that person was you, it'd be too much. But I think it's just right for me," Tiffany responded. Kim let out a sympathetic laugh.

"Did I tell you all that I may have a stalker?" Tiffany asked, changing the subject.

"What?" Kim gasped.

"Do you think it's Richard?" Jillian asked nonchalantly. She didn't even bother to look up. She was certain now that Tommie's suspicions were correct.

"I don't think its Richard, but truthfully, I cannot tell you *who* it is. I don't have any suspects. But since I ran him through the ringer, it wouldn't surprise me. But, I really don't think it's him."

"Why aren't you staying with Tommie?" Jillian inquired.

"Girl, I'm not about to let some fool run me out of my home."

Tiffany pulled into her three-car garage and Maria ran from the house. She ran to the driver's side and reached in to hug Tiffany before she could get out of the truck. She then made her rounds to Jillian and then Kim.

"We are some beautiful women aren't we?" she asked taking them all in. They were in fact, beautiful, successful and well-rounded women.

Kim and Jillian grabbed their luggage and the ladies went into the house. Tiffany was the last one in.

"Okay, let's hurry up. Tommie said she'll be in here about twenty minutes." The ladies scrambled into the house and made sure everything was in order for their friend's surprise birthday party. Maria had done a great job hanging streamers and blowing up balloons.

"I sure hope you know you're cleaning up all this confetti you've spread all over my house," Tiffany said.

They all laughed as Jillian uncovered the cake. "I think I'm going to leave the candles off this cake. If Tommie comes in here and sees forty candles on her birthday cake, she just might flip."

"I think you right," Kim said as she uncovered the rest of the food. Maria made sure there was plenty of wine and drinks.

"Maria, thank you so much for getting in early and taking care of this. Tommie told me she was going to visit Captain Lane's grave today. I'm not sure what kind of mood she'll be in when she gets here, so I want to make sure we're there for her," Tiffany said.

Twenty-Two

Tommie had planned on visiting her father's gravesite, something she'd done every year on her birthday. As she was in route, she received a call on her cell phone from Captain Randall.

"I know you've got plans, and I'll try to make this as quick is possible, but I need you to come in as soon as possible."

"Please don't tell me the HRB has struck again."

"Just get here," the Captain reiterated.

Tommie turned her SUV around and followed her Captain's instructions. She would have to wait to have her yearly conversation with her dead father's tombstone. She was praying that none one else had fallen victim to Lucien's crime spree.

When she got to the prescient, Tommie dropped her bag on her desk and marched straight into Captain Randall's office.

"What's going on Captain," she asked.

"Shut the door and have a seat," the Captain instructed her, as he made sure the blinds to his office were closed. "I didn't want John anywhere near this, take a look." The Captain used a remote to turn on the large flat screen television that hung on the wall.

"Breaking news from KUSA Channel 9." A reporter was standing in the middle of a crime scene with several police officers and first responders. A medical examiners truck could be seen in the background. "Police here have discovered the body of former District Attorney Michael Warren. Michael Warren assisted in efforts to convict, accused murderer, Lucien Guillory back in the late nineties. Lucien Guillory who served nearly fifteen years in a Colorado corrections facility was released from prison last year after winning an appeal, resulting in an overturned verdict. Suspicion has loomed after the judge who officiated over the case was found dead along with several of the jurors that served on the jury were found murdered late last month. According to our records, Lucien Guillory still resides in the Denver Metro area and has been in touch with the judicial system on a weekly basis. Wait . . . we're getting word that the Chief of Police, Robert White will give a press conference in just a few minutes."

Tommie and Captain Randall watched as people scrambled about the crime scene in preparation of the news conference. A few moments later Chief White took to the makeshift podium and gave details of the new findings.

Captain Randall ended the recorded video and shut off the television. "Now, I don't know about you, but I'm one-hundred percent sure that Lucien Guillory is behind this."

"I am too," Tommie agreed. "The police chief said that an eye witness said they saw a suspicious looking green Ford Fusion with Colorado license plate KEI7LT0 speed away from that area."

"Right. We need to run those plates, but I'll venture to say that someone saw something much more than a suspicious car driving away." Captain Randall made reference to the expensive apartment buildings and high rises that surrounded the area. "That place is lit up like a Christmas Tree."

"Well there's not much we can do pertaining to what they found there, but I'm going to run the plates on that car. There's something that I'm still having a hard time connecting with."

"What?"

"Well, it's becoming apparent that Lucien is trying to kill everyone that had anything to do with his case. But I'm not sure what these spiritual leaders have to do with anything. And, Tiffany and I were like daughters to him. That's what I don't get."

"Well, maybe we have more than one mole," Captain Randall suggested.

"Trust me, that thought has already crossed my mind."

"Meaning?"

"Captain, I have a strong hunch that one of my girlfriends knows more than she's saying."

"Which one?"

"Jillian."

"That's the one that lives in Denver right?"

"Yes. I know she knew about Lucien's release, but she failed to tell me. She claims she knew nothing about it and that she's had no contact with him. I know she's lying."

The captain stood up, walked around his desk and sat on the edge. "Go ahead and run those plates and I will see what I can find on Jillian Dawson. Once you run those plates, I don't want to see you back in here until next week—unless of course, Lucien strikes again."

Tommie nodded in agreement, sat down at her desk and entered the required information into her computer. She waited for the computer to give results. When they came back, she printed them out and went into Captain Randall's office.

"Those plates came back to a Dollar Car Rental at Denver International Airport. It was rented to a Paige Guillory but was returned this morning. I'm running a trace on this Paige Guillory to see if we can come up with something." She sat the print out on her boss's desk and promised she'd try not to see him until Monday.

Tommie left the precinct and headed towards her father's gravesite once more. She may have been hit with a minor setback, having to go into the precinct, but nothing was going to stop her from visiting her father. It had been her ritual since his death.

When she got near her father's resting place, she sat in the car for a moment and looked around the cemetery. Cemeteries had given her the creeps as a child and still did as an adult. She tried to focus only on her father's grave and pretend that he was the only one here. Captain Lane was buried near an old magnolia tree. Even though she knew better, Tommie felt that her father enjoyed the beautiful trees and couldn't wait for its yearly bloom.

Today, she wasn't the only person in the cemetery. To her right, she could see other families across the site, with their children visiting various plots. To her left, she could see a burial service going on. Luckily the grounds were large enough that no one was disturbed.

Tommie picked up the flower basket that sat in the passenger side of her truck and exited the vehicle. Her father's space was only a few feet ahead as she made her way to his grave. She kneeled down, and as she begin to strategically place the fresh flowers, she began a conversation with her father.

"Good afternoon father. I'm sorry I'm late. You know me, all work and no play. I really wished you were here for this one. You wouldn't believe it, but Lucien Guillory is out of jail and wreaking havoc. He's killed so many people since he's been out and now, I think—no, I'm sure, he's after the girls and I. Don't ask me how he got out, something about Miranda rights and confessions. I don't really care. Our judicial system is so messed up. The fact still remains that he killed mom, he should be rotting in that prison."

Tommie stopped for a moment when she could hear a faint wail from the left where the burial service was going on. She could certainly understand how the wailing woman felt. Knowing how it felt to bury someone you love, knowing she'd never seem them again made Tommie queasy.

"I feel a little off my game. I feel Lucien has been toying with me. He's killed across three states. I should have had him by now."

She looked at the empty plot next to her fathers. This was where she had made plans to be buried. She had wished that her mother could be buried here too, but that was not in the plans. She tried to take her mind off the empty plot and focused on her father's tombstone. It read:

Captain Euliss Lane August 19, 1946 – May 7, 1998. Service, Integrity and Love. You are one of God's greatest treasures. May you rest in the peace of God. John 3:16.

Tommie talked to her father a little while longer before kneeling down and giving the headstone her ritualistic kiss and saying a prayer.

"I love you daddy. May your soul be at rest and I pray that we'll see each other again." With that Tommie got back into her SUV and exited the cemetery.

Tommie pulled into Tiffany's driveway about thirty minutes later. She knew there would be no room in the garage, so she walked around to the front door and put her key in the lock.

"Okay. Shush. Here she comes," Tiffany told the other girls. They all hid and waited for Tommie to enter the house.

Tommie opened the front door, disabled the alarm and walked through the foyer, past Tiffany's office and past the formal living room into the kitchen. The ladies could hear her shoes clank against the hardwood floors. Tommie looked around and when she didn't see anyone, she said, "Where are those reality rejects?"

Just as she rounded the corner, she saw the decorations and before she could say anything, her girlfriends appeared from various directions.

"Surprise!" they all said.

"Who you call real reject?" Kim asked giving her friend a hug. They all laughed. No one understood why Kim talked with an Asian accent when she was born in the United States.

"You guys know I don't like surprises and I don't need any reminders of my age."

"Well I guess I had better take all forty-two of those candles off the cake," Jillian mumbled.

"I'm only forty smarty pants," Tommie defended herself. All the women burst into laughter.

"Ah, you guys are the best. I wouldn't trade either of you for anything in this world."

"Now let's eat. I'm hungry," Maria said.

"You're always hungry," Tiffany said picking a large shrimp out of the pasta salad Tiffany had made.

It was the first time in months that the girlfriends had partaken in their regular girl's weekend and it was long overdue. Typically, the ladies would have a girl's getaway on a monthly basis, rotating between San Diego, Greensboro, Key West and Denver. Occasionally the ladies would escape to Vegas, take in the sights, do a little gambling, and eat all the food they could stand.

This time they would visit the Biltmore House in Asheville, the Outer Banks—mainly Wrightsville Beach, the newly remodeled Civil Rights Museum in downtown Greensboro, the North Carolina State Zoo and to top it all off, they would head out to Myrtle Beach.

The women had all been the graduating class of 1987 at Montbello High School in Denver. They were childhood friends and shared a special bond. They had a pact—they'd be close friends forever and now, they had so much catching up to do.

A size four, Maria Santiago stood five-foot eight. She was Puerto Rican and had flawless cocoa skin. She only wore a hint of makeup—tinted lip gloss and mascara. She had lightened her brunette locks, which nearly came to her waist. Her green eyes only added to her alluring beauty.

After graduation, Maria left Denver to attend UC Berkley. There she received a Bachelors in Information Technology and then a Masters in Communication. Months before she even graduated, she was offered a position at SPAWAR (Space and Naval Warfare Systems Command) in Key West, Florida as a Corporate Operations Lead. After much hard work and proving to be an asset to the organization, Jennifer was promoted to Director of Office of Counsel.

Kim Pham had moved to San Diego, California after her parents had disowned her. She was Vietnamese and her family did not approve of her dating outside her race. She had always dated black men, and after her family found out she was pregnant by one, they ousted her from the family and the family fortune.

All the stress was, inevitably, too much for Kim. She lost the child during her third trimester of pregnancy. The child's father was long gone—he had received a scholarship to play football at Nebraska State University.

With no ties keeping her in Denver, Kim moved to San Diego where she attended San Diego State. She received her Master's in Business with a concentration in marketing. Kim went on to become of the most successful dot com creators. SocialStat was started in a rented office space in Sorrento Valley, California by just her and a college roommate.

SocialStat had expanded from its original nine-hundred square feet to fifty-thousand square feet and from two employees to twenty-five employees. SocialStat was the third largest social media platform in the world. Not bad for a woman who had been blacklisted from the family's fortune.

Jillian Dawson was a late bloomer. After all the other girls had gone off to college, Jillian stayed in Denver to take care of her ailing father. He had been diagnosed with testicular cancer towards the end of their high school year.

Jillian never admitted it, but she was envious that her friends were off to the colleges of their choices while she was left behind to attend Metro Community College, while taking care of a sick father. She loved her father, but this was supposed to be her time to leave the nest, find herself and blossom into a successful woman.

She finally caught a break after her father's death. She received her Bachelor's at Colorado State University in Information Technology. Even though she loved her girls, Jillian still held an unknown grudge against the women.

"You need a haircut Mamacita?" Maria said bluntly.

"I told you she was a hot mess," Tiffany said. "But we're going to change that. We've got a spa day set up, complete with massages, hair and nails."

"You know I hate that bourgeois crap," Tommie said.

Tiffany touched the top of Tommie's head and ran her fingers through her hair. "Trust me honey, you need it. There are so many naps in that kitchen to start another World War!" All the ladies laughed, except for Jillian.

"Hello Jillian," Tommie said.

"Happy Birthday," Jillian answered, her delivery a phony as a three-dollar-bill.

Tommie looked around the kitchen and the great room. "I'm thinking Tiffany must not be feeling well," she said.

"Why do you say that?" Tiffany asked.

"You let them decorate? There's confetti, balloons and streamers everywhere."

"Now you know, they'll be cleaning it up before long. Because if I have to clean it up, I'm renting out their rooms," Tiffany joked. They all laughed.

"I am so hungry, what is that smell?" Tommie asked, eying the spread on counter. All of her favorites were displayed before her; shrimp pasta salad, thin crust pizza, chimichangas, fried rice and an array of other goodies. She eyed the birthday cake. It was in the shape of a gun and a badge and read:

Detective Tommie Lane: Greensboro's Finest.

Immediately Tommie recognized the maker of the cake. "I'd know Sebastian's cakes anywhere. How did you get him to make one on such short notice?"

"It wasn't short notice," Tiffany answered. "I've been working with Sebastian for a while, trying to get this cake just right. I must say he did a great job."

"He did an *awesome* job. I've always wanted one of his cakes."

"Who Sebastian?" Kim asked.

"He's only the greatest cake designer in the Triad."

"Girl don't let Sebastian hear you call him that. Call him the Cake Boss!" Tiffany said as he pulled up the cake maker's website on her iPad mini. She showed it to Kim.

"Wow. He do good job."

"Yes he does!" Tiffany agreed.

The ladies grabbed plates of food and glasses of wine and headed to the great room. Tiffany turned on her Bose radio system, allowing smooth Jazz sounds to surround the room.

"Tiffany, why do you have this big old house, when it's just you?" Jillian asked looking around the immaculate great room. "It looks like you never come in here."

Tiffany took in a deep breath. If Jillian said one more thing about her house, she was going to let her have it. But, it was Tommie's birthday and it had been a while since she spent time with the women she was most closest to, so she let it go. "Actually, the only time I do come in here is when you guys are here. Otherwise, this room sees no action."

"If you'd let me set you up, all your rooms would be getting a little action," Tommie smirked.

"You need to be trying to get action for yourself, Charlotte's Web!" Tiffany shot back. More laughter.

"Good one. You got me," Tommie said.

The ladies dug into their dinner, drank wine and reminisced.

"So you tell us about break in?" Kim asked. Everyone stopped what they were doing and stared at Tiffany.

"I thought I told you not to tell anyone," Tommie said.

"I know but these are my girls," Tiffany defended.

"I know but, the least amount of people who know the better chances we have of finding this creep."

"Well the cat out of bag, now," Kim said. "What happen?" Tommie opened up the floor for Tiffany to speak.

"For a while now, I've been getting this creepy feeling. As if someone is in the house when I'm here. It feels as if they've been watching me. After inspector Tommie here went through the house, it appears, someone has been entering the house through one of the windows and hiding out in the attic." All the women gasped—all except for Jillian. "Can you believe that? I just had this house built."

"It's time to move," Maria said.

"I'm not letting some dirt bag scare me from my home. There's no way in hell."

"It's too big anyway," Jillian mumbled.

"Too big for who?" Tiffany asked. She had had just about enough.

"I'm just saying," Jillian tried to defend herself.

"Why are you so worried about how big my house is? I paid for it with *my* money." Tiffany was getting heated. She thought back and it seemed that Jillian always had something to say about anything that she bought. When Tiffany bought her fully loaded Range Rover, Jillian said it was too much to pay for a car. When Tiffany bought a one-hundred-thousand dollar pair of diamond studs, Jillian said she was showboating. She loved Jillian, but it was none of her business what she did with her money.

"I'm waiting to hear it Jillian Paige Dawson! Why are you so worried about what I do with my money?"

"Okay, okay. Let's chill out . . . ," Tommie said. "Wait a minute, what did you just say?" she asked Tiffany.

"Huh?" Tiffany said.

"Jillian your middle name *is* Paige isn't it?" Tiffany and Tommie looked at each other startled. They gave each that knowing look that only the two of them shared. Tiffany nodded at Tommie as if she knew what her next move would be.

Tommie gave a nervous laugh and said, “Actually Tiffany, I think Jillian could take you,” she said trying to change the mood. Everyone looked puzzled.

Tiffany chuckled and said, “You’re probably right because I’m a lover, not a fighter.”But it was a facade. Just like Tommie, Tiffany was positive that their childhood friend Jillian was actually one Paige Guillory.

“So speaking of men, Jillian, are you seeing someone?” Kim asked.

“Well, not really. Don’t act like you guys can’t tell I’ve gained weight.”

“So what Mami,” Maria said. “Men love women with meat on their bones.”

“What about you Maria,” Jillian asked trying to deflect the question.

“No, not me. I can’t seem to find a man who doesn’t need a green card.” She made circle motions around her body, “How’s he going to handle all of this if he can’t even get his own green card?” The laughs kept coming.

Twenty-three

The ladies ate the rest of their dinner, drank more wine and talked about the good old days before deciding to watch *Bridesmaids* which starred Melissa McCarthy, Kristen Wig and Mya Rudolph. The movie reminded the ladies of themselves, except none of them were getting married.

About midway through the movie, Tiffany, noticed that Jillian had not come back from her bathroom excursion, so she went to make sure she was okay. She stopped in her tracks when she heard Jillian on the phone.

"They're getting too close. We need to do it as soon as possible."

Tiffany wasn't too sure who she was talking to, but she had an idea. She listened for a moment to Jillian's unsavory conversation.

Tiffany cleared her throat in an effort to let Jillian know she was about to round the corner. Suddenly Jillian changed her tune.

"Yes, I'll have the report in your email next week," Jillian said loud and upbeat. She told the person she was talking to goodbye and ended the call.

"Everything okay?" Tiffany asked her.

"Oh yea. That was Rick. Every time I go on vacation, they act like they can't function without me," she chuckled patting Tiffany on the shoulder.

Tiffany didn't believe her. "Well you know, you can talk to me if you need to. I've noticed that you've been a bit distant since I picked you up from the airport."

"It's nothing really. Maybe a little stress at work. Don't get me wrong, I love what I do, but it can be daunting at times."

"Well okay, but remember, my door is always open." The two ladies hugged. "No let's get back to the movie, because that Melissa McCarthy is hilarious. I'm still trying to figure out which one is me," Tiffany said.

"I think you're Melissa McCarthy," Jillian said.

"And I think you're Kristen Wig," Tiffany laughed.

With arms linked, the two ladies returned to the great room. No one noticed their re-entry into the room . . . except for Tommie. She, too, had made note of Jillian's attitude. Now that she knew who her friend really was, she made a mental note to keep an eye on her. She texted Captain Randall.

Know who Paige Guillory is. Found 2nd mole. Run jacket Jillian Paige Dawson.

After the movie, the women, laughed hysterically, drank wine and told stories of themselves as if they were to make their own movie.

"My story would be a romantic love story like the Titanic," Maria said, using her some-timey Puerto Rican voice. "Except it would be a little different. Like when the boat went down and Leonardo put Kate on the drifting wood, I'd be like, get on this piece of wood Papi. You can get on top of me, because I'm going to need someone to pay the bills if we make it out of this. No, no. I would have pushed one of the other Mamacitas off their wood just to make sure my Pablo survived," she concluded.

"That is just wrong," the ladies said in unison.

"Yea, and Tommie here would be Detective Benson in Law and Order: SVU. If Detective Stabler was my partner, I know what I'd do," Tiffany said.

"I already have a partner—John," Tommie said.

The ladies got quiet for a few seconds and looked around at each other.

Then a rupture of laughter broke out from everyone except for Jillian.

"You're a fool!" Tiffany said, with tears falling from her eyes. "John, oh my goodness!"

"He is my partner and you all know John is nowhere near my type."

"I glad you clean up, I was starting to worry about you," Kim said.

"Kim would play Lucy Lu in Charlie's Angels," Tommie suggested.

"Why I can no play Pam Grier in like Foxy Brown you sucka!" Kim said as she took her Foxy Brown stance. Another eruption of laughter.

"Oh my goodness, I cannot remember the last time we laughed like this," Maria said. "I love you guys." The ladies huddled into a group hug.

After their embrace, Maria had made it to the kitchen island to refill her plate with pasta and her wine glass with Moscato. She lifted her glass and said, "To love, happiness, and all that other . . . umm, stuff."

"Here, here," the ladies all said lifting their glasses.

Twenty-four

Greensboro, NC
Friday, August 31, 2012

The next morning, the ladies were awakened to the smell of bacon, eggs, homemade waffles and coffee. They had no idea that Lucien had snuck into the house and previewed their comedic theatrics. They didn't know that Jillian and Lucien had made love in her guest room. It was after six o'clock in the morning when Lucien woke up and realized the time. He knew if he didn't get out of the house as soon as possible, his cover would be blown.

"Where did you order this food from Tiffany?" Jillian said walking into kitchen in her lingerie.

"Well good morning to you, *too*. If I didn't know any better, I'd say you got you some last night," Tiffany teased her. Jillian's face became flushed.

"What do you mean?" Had Tiffany known that Lucien had slept in her room just hours earlier, she'd have a heart attack.

"I mean, you're glowing and your demeanor has done a complete one-eighty since last night. And besides, who wears Frederick's of Hollywood to a girls sleepover?"

"How do you know this is Frederick's? You can't fit anything in Frederick's."

"If I know anything about lingerie, I know Victoria Secrets and Frederick's of Hollywood. And Frederick's is not *just* for plus sized women.

Jillian breathed a sigh of relief. "You know, I'm just trying to find a way to feel good about myself again."

"Honey chile, you are beautiful, don't let anyone tell you different. You're a gorgeous white girl and you've got a whole lot of junk in your trunk. If you ask me, you're a triple threat to most black women," Tiffany said.

"What?"

"I mean, black men already like white girls—that's one. Then your hair is the *real* Yaki straight number three-twenty-seven—that's two, and then to have a white girl with junk in her trunk? *Giirrrl*, you've got it made. You know brothers can't resist a woman with junk in her trunk, no matter what color she is. So the way I see it Miss Jillian, if I had a boyfriend *or* husband, I'd keep him as far away from you as I possibly could."

Jillian thought that was probably the nicest thing anyone had ever said to her. She walked around the kitchen island, gave Tiffany a hug and said "Thank you." Tiffany saw Tommie over Jillian's shoulder.

"Morning divas," Tommie said. "Tiffany, I see you had the food delivered. That must be what I heard early this morning. I could have sworn, I heard one of the exterior doors open and shut. And then I heard someone outside . . . almost as if they were whispering."

Jillian became tense. She knew there wasn't too much anyone could get past Tommie. "In this big old . . ." she started, but when she noticed Tiffany's glare, she restated her words. "I mean, the house is big and new and it could be that it's settling and making noise. That's all I was going to say." Tiffany smiled at her and then gave Tommie a knowing glance.

They both knew that if Tommie heard something that wasn't right, it probably wasn't. They both concluded in their minds that Lucien had been in the house. For all they knew, he could still be in the house, watching them.

Maria and Kim joined the ladies in the kitchen. "*Ooh*, you order take out for breakfast?" Kim asked.

"Probably Mimi's Cafe," Tommie mumbled.

"Excuse me, you ingrates," Tiffany said, becoming irritated. "I'll have you know that I cooked every last bit of this food here from scratch, including the *dam*n waffles. I *can* cook you know. I *was* married to Richard for all those years." The girls broke out in laughter.

"And we all knew that you didn't cook for Richard either. That's why he had so many mistresses—one to cook, one to . . ." Jillian realized she had gone too far. Tiffany reminded herself to punch Jillian in the face when no one was looking.

"Hey Tommie, I heard you visited the Captain's gravesite yesterday. How did that go?" Maria asked. She knew that if she didn't defuse the situation, that someone would be probably end up getting hurt. Her bet was on Tiffany, but Jillian had gained a few pounds since she'd seen her last, so she wasn't so sure.

"It was nice, actually. I put fresh flowers on his tombstone. He's probably rolling over, cursing me out, wondering why I'm still on the force and not married yet. He always talked about the grandchildren I was going to give him. You know, I'm really not interested in getting married, but I do want a child to carry on my mother and father's legacy after I'm gone. After all, I am an only child and once I'm gone, the bloodline stops there."

"I can understand that," Maria said. "But you're only forty, that's the new twenty. I'm sure you'll find love sometime soon, and if not, women get . . . what's that thing that women do when they want to have a child and they have their pick of sperm donors?"

"Artificial insemination," Tiffany confirmed.

"Yes that's it. You could always do that. They even have it where, now, you can pick the sex of the child, the color of their eyes and other features," Maria continued.

"I don't like playing with God like that. I might be creating a serial killer to go or something." Tommie noticed Jillian's face turn beet red, but she didn't acknowledge her.

"We'll see," Tommie said. "God's will, be done."

All the ladies said "Amen" and dug into breakfast.

After eating a few bites of her egg white omelet, Kim said, "You lie Tiff. No way you cook this breakfast. It's so good." The ladies erupted in laughter while Tiffany rolled her eyes and threw a strawberry at Kim.

Twenty-Five

After breakfast, the ladies decided on an excursion to the zoo and from there, they'd head to the spa.

"I think it's a good idea were going to the zoo early. Because once it gets hot, no one is going to want to do *anything*." Tommie said. Although Tommie had been to the zoo once before, she never got a chance to explore the entire park. She had received a police call in the middle of her tour.

"I hate to sound selfish ladies, but can we visit the African Pavilion first?" Tommie asked. "That's on the other side."

The ladies agreed and made their way to a nearby tour trolley and headed to the other side of the animal park. Once they got to the other side of the park, they enjoyed the plants and trees in the Tropical Plant Walk Exhibit.

"Alligator Pepper? What in the world?" Tiffany asked. She read the description to the girls. "Alligator pepper is one of West Africa's most frequently used medical plants. Leaves, stems, roots and fruit are used to treat many illnesses and are also added to magnify the effects of other medical plants. The leaves are used to wrap food before cooking and also in soups and stews to impart flavor. All parts of the plan have a sweet pepper smell."

She bent down to smell the interesting plant. "Hmm, it has a distinct smell to it, but it's not sweet."

"I've never hear of it," Kim chimed in.

The ladies chatted about the various other plants they passed and had never heard of, like the African Oil Palm and the Coffee Tree.

They got real excited when they passed a baboon exhibit.

"Ha-muh-dry-ass," Kim said trying to pronounce a type of baboon. The girls broke out in laughter.

"Don't laugh at me," Kim said. "Let me see one of you try to pronounce that.

"It's Ha-muh-dry-us," Tommie said.

"You're actually right," the tour guide confirmed and then proceeded to give the ladies the history of the Hamadryas Baboon.

The tour bus took them to the far end of the exhibit and let them off so they could enjoy themselves as they made their way back to their starting point.

"I sure hope you all wore comfortable shoes, because there's going to be a whole lot of walking going on," Tommie informed them.

In unison, the ladies confirmed that they had come prepared with appropriate walking shoes and made sure they had a bottle of water and a piece of fruit in their purses.

The ladies explored the exhibits, stopping to talk to various animals and make funny gestures at them. The all took photos. Before they knew it, they were back at the plant exhibit, where they explored Calabash Nutmeg, African Violets, Orchards and a Swizzle Stick Tree. Before they knew it, they were right back where they had started in the middle of the park.

"Whew, my feet are telling me to sit down a bit," Tiffany said.

"I'm hungry," Jillian said.

"So am I," Maria chimed in.

"You're always hungry!" the girls shouted.

The girls looked through the brochures they had received when they entered the park and look for somewhere to eat.

"How about the Wilderness Cafe or the Junction Springs Cafe?" Tommie suggested.

"I don't care, just as long as there is shade," Tiffany said.

The ladies unanimously agreed on Junction Springs Cafe and agreed to head over to Cool Play for some cool Dippin' Dots.

Once they had their food and were seated, they gobbled down their treats and indulged in small talk.

"So Kim, how is SocialStat doing?" Tiffany asked Kim. "I'm on that network more than Facebook *and* Twitter."

"You know, it go really well. I find out last week we reach seventeen point five million users," Kim beamed with proud.

"Wow that's more than Twitter!" Maria said excitedly.

"Yes, but we want to check and recheck the data before announce that we are number two."

"Hey in the social media game, I'll take number two any day," Tiffany said.

Tommie noticed that Jillian was awfully quiet. Actually, she hadn't said much the entire trip. Tommie looked at Tiffany who acted as if she could read her mind. Tiffany nodded her head.

"So Jillian, how are things coming along for you?" Tiffany asked.

"Things are good," Jillian responded dryly.

"Just *good*?" Tiffany asked. She wasn't letting Jillian off that easily. "You're the go-to IT person for one of the top brokerage firms in the country. I'd say that's more than just okay."

Tommie threw daggers at Tiffany and jumped in on the interrogation.

"Didn't you mention a while back that you enrolled at the University of Phoenix to get your Masters?"

"Uh, yea, well, I did, but things got too busy, so I dropped my classes. Besides, the University of Phoenix is nothing compared to the prestigious schools you ladies went to," Jillian said holding her head down in embarrassment.

"Excuse me honey, but where do you think I'm currently obtaining my doctorate as we speak? University of Phoenix! I take classes on line, and once a week, I hike my fanny right up to the satellite campus by the mall. I have nine months left and then I am done." Tiffany nodded her head towards Jillian for emphasis and popped a couple of Dippin' Dots in her mouth.

"Jillian, what happened to you?" Tommie finally asked.

"What do you mean?"

"I mean, you're so down on yourself lately and your self-esteem all but exists. I'm not downing you about your weight gain, but why not own it? I think you look fabulous, but ever since you've been here you've made reference to your weight and every chance you get, you put yourself down."

Jillian's face turned red as she looked around at each of the ladies and then put her head back down. "I'll be alright, I just need to lose some weight," was all she said.

"You don't need to lose no weight Mami," Maria said. "And if you want to give some weight away, give some to Kim, she could stand to gain some weight."

"Hey, I like the way I am," Kim injected and playfully slapped Maria in the shoulder. The two laughed and hugged each other.

As much as she despised Jillian right now, Tiffany took her hand and asked, "Is your boyfriend beating you?"

Jillian's head shot straight up. "Boyfriend? What are you talking about? I don't have a boyfriend," she shouted in panic.

"Calm down! Calm down!" Tommie said, looking around at the audience who now watched them.

"I didn't mean to upset you," Tiffany said. "I'm just concerned about you."

"Don't worry about me," Jillian huffed. "I'll be just fine," she said and rolled her eyes.

Tiffany squinted her eyes towards Tommie as Tommie stared Jillian down. Jillian was up for the challenge but put her head down when Tommie dropped a bombshell on them.

"So I told you guys about this case I've been working on right?"

All the ladies nodded. "Yes, Holy Roller Bandit right?" Kim asked.

"Yes, that's the one," Tommie confirmed. Although Tommie was not looking at Jillian at that moment, she knew Jillian was looking at her, and Tiffany's facial expression confirmed that.

"So what's going on with the case Tommie. Have you guys caught this creep yet?" Maria asked.

"Not yet, but we're close. We found out where he's been living," she said.

Jillian choked on her Dippin' Dots. "What?" she asked.

"Yes, he's been living in Atlanta the whole time," Tommie said. Jillian took a deep breath.

"Wow," Maria said. "Why is he in Greensboro killing people?"

"We still haven't figured that part out yet, but I bet you guys wouldn't guess in a million years who he is?"

The girls looked around at each other puzzled.

"Is he someone we went to school with?" Tiffany asked, pretending not to know the answer. "You know Chuck went to jail for killing that girl?"

"No, much, much, *much* closer," Tommie said.

"*Who*?" Tiffany asked, adding emphasis. "You're killing us over here."

"Dad," Tommie said in a low tone, making sure no one else around them could hear.

"Dad who?" Tiffany asked.

"Lucien," Tommie said. Jillian gasped loudly, as if she was going to have a heart attack.

"Lucien who?" Maria asked. "I know you're not talking about Lucien Guillory, because Lucien Guillory killed mom and that bastard is in jail, and that's where he'll rot."

"This is not funny Tommie," Kim chimed in.

"I would never joke about something like this," Tommie assured her.

"Get out of here," Tiffany said.

"What in the world?" Maria asked, while Kim just sat there with her mouth wide open.

"How did you find this out?" Jillian finally asked.

"Well, I can't give away all the details of the case because the investigation is still ongoing. But I do know that when Lucien was let out of jail, the courts were required to contact all parties involved and make them aware of his release." Tommie paused for a moment. "Well I never received my notification. Ironically, out of the blue, his sister sent me a message on SocialStat. I mean, I knew Lucien had sisters, but I never really met them. They sought me out and found me on SocialStat." Tommie smiled at Kim.

"Anyway," Tommie continued, "she told me that Lucien had been released on a technicality." All the women gasped.

"Hey Jillian, did you know he was being released? Did they notify you? Was there anything on the news or in the papers about it?" Tiffany asked.

"Why the hell are you guys asking me? I don't know anything about it," Jillian said getting defensive.

"Wow Mami, what has you so on edge? It was only a question," Maria said rolling her eyes at Jillian.

"I'm sorry. This stress at work is just taking its toll on me. This promotion at work requires a lot more responsibility, which means a lot more stress," Jillian said.

"A promotion?" Tommie said trying to sound excited for her backstabbing friend. "Why didn't you tell us? Congratulations! I'm so excited for you."

The ladies gathered around Jillian and gave her a group hug. And after a few minutes of praise, they focused their attention back to Tommie's case.

"So Tommie, how are you dealing with the fact that Lucien is the one behind all these murders? And why is he killing people in Greensboro of all . . .?" Maria asked. But, before she could get her last words out, Jillian collapsed, her body folding over the wooden bench she had been sitting on, coming to a rest on the hot cement. Immediately the ladies jumped into action as they all gathered around Jillian. Bystanders stood by in disbelief.

Tiffany took a small towel from her bag and put it under Jillian's head before sprinkling water on her face and neck. "I'm sure she's overheated and exhausted," she said.

Tommie placed her index and middle fingers against Jillian's neck. She was still breathing. She took out her cell phone and dialed 911. "We need a bus at the NC Zoo . . . South side of the Africa Exhibit . . . food court . . . female . . . approximately thirty-nine . . . possible heat exhaustion . . ."

One of the restaurant owners offered to have Jillian come inside their establishment where it was cooler. The ladies all pitched in and helped Jillian inside. She was alert, but her skin was red and clammy and she was sweating profusely.

"I'm okay," she finally said. "I'm just hot. I can't believe how hot it is." She nearly fell again before the ladies sat her down in a nearby chair.

Maria looked at the Accu-Weather app on her cell phone. The temperature was eighty-one degrees. "Are you pregnant?" she asked Jillian.

At the sound of Maria's question, Jillian appeared to be losing consciousness.

"Are you pregnant Jill?" Maria asked her again.

"Why you keep ask that?" Kim asked. Tommie looked at Tiffany. They didn't know how they missed the signs.

"That explains a lot. I'm going to go out on a limb and say she *is* pregnant. I don't know how we missed it."

Tommie fanned Jillian's face with her tour guide program. "Jillian, how far along are you?" Jillian could only let out a moan. "Jillian, it's important that you tell us how far along you are. We have to make sure the baby is getting enough oxygen."

"Four months," she said faintly.

"She's getting hotter," Tiffany panicked. All the ladies used their tour guide programs to fan their ailing friend. A few moments later, a man, who appeared to be the park ranger, escorted paramedics inside the cool structure.

Tommy explained to them that she fainted and advised that she was pregnant. She told them she was a detective with the Greensboro Police Department and verified that they would take her to Moses Cone.

"Moses Cone? They can't take her to Wesley Long?" Tiffany asked. "You know how bad Moses Cone is."

"Right now we don't have a choice," Tommie said.

"I wouldn't send my worst enemy to Moses Cone," Tiffany mumbled.

*****

When the ladies reached the emergency room to check Jillian's status, the doctor would only talk to Tommie. She informed Tommie that Jillian would be okay but she had to stay a couple of days in the hospital.

"She's suffering from a little heat exhaustion and anxiety. Has she been stressed out about anything? It's more than likely taking its toll on her," the doctor said. Tommie told her she didn't know because her friend lived out of state, but Tommie knew exactly what it was that had Jillian stressed out.

"What about the baby?" Tommie asked her.

"The baby is alright for now. There was a little bleeding, but we've managed to stop it. She's going to need to stay off her feet for a while. She may even have to go on complete bed rest until she has the baby. I'm waiting for the results back on the pregnancy test to see how far along she is."

"I believe she is either three or four months," Tommie informed the doctor.

"We'll know for sure when the tests come back. They will give us a better gage on what she needs and what the baby needs."

"Thanks doctor," Tommie said. She returned to the waiting room where the girls were waiting.

"How is she," they asked in unison.

"She'll be fine. The doctor may have to put her on bed rest for a while." Tommie relayed to the ladies what the doctor had told her.

"Why we not know she was pregnant?" Kim asked.

"There are a lot of things you all don't know. But, for your safety, I'm going to have to level with you all."

"What are you talking about Mami?" Maria asked.

"Let me take care of things here and then I will tell you once we get back to Tiffany's."

"Are they keeping her?" Tiffany asked.

"Yes," Tommie answered. "For a couple of days. They have to make sure she and the baby are okay. And I guess it forces her to get some rest. It'll also keep her out of our hair for the next couple of days. Let's see Lucien try to get by without her." Just as Tommie spoke those words, Jillian's cell phone chimed with the *Against All Odds* by Phil Collins ringtone.

"Is that her phone?" Tommie asked Tiffany who was holding Jillian's purse.

"I didn't hear anything," Tiffany said, but just then, the phone rang louder. "I guess it is," she said removing it from her friend's purse.

"Let me have it," Tommie demanded. She answered the phone, but no one said anything. She knew who it was. "I know it's you Lucien. You don't have to say a word, just listen. I can guarantee you that I will have gotten you long before this poor baby is born. Chess is not one of your strong suits. I'm coming for you and I'm going to hunt you down like the rabid dog you are. And we know what they do to rabid dogs," she said before the phone went dead.

"Was that him?" Tiffany asked.

"I'm sure it was," Tommy responded. "Give me a minute, I'm working on security detail for Jillian. I can guarantee you, he will come looking for her. It's not like Greensboro has a plethora of hospitals. He *will* find her. I don't want him going anywhere near her."

Tommie secured security detail for Jillian and advised the staff that by no uncertain terms was anyone allowed to enter the room, unless they were a doctor or other police personnel and everyone needed to sign in with the security guards outside her door before entering the room.

After she was sure that Jillian was safe, she and the other ladies headed back to Tiffany's house.

Twenty-Six

Before entering Tiffany's home, Tommie made sure the house was secure.

Once inside, Maria finally said, "Look, what's going on? Some pretty strange things have been going on."

"Let's just pray for Jillian. That baby is going to need her to get strong," Tommie said. Then she held her index finger to her lips advising the women to be silent, as she pulled out her iPad. She used hand gestures and instructed the ladies to do the same. The miniature tablets were a gift from Kim. They all were branded with the SocialStat and Apple logos.

The ladies followed Tiffany into her office while Tommy drew her gun and searched every inch of the house making sure locks, doors and windows were secured.

When Tommie returned to Tiffany's office, she nodded towards Tiffany who removed one of the many books she had in her immaculate book shelving. It was Pride and Prejudice. She opened the hollow book, took out a remote and pressed it. The ladies were amazed when a small section of the bookcase slid open.

The entrance was very narrow. Had Jillian been with them, she would not have been able to get through the entry way. Once the ladies were secure in Tiffany's panic room—one of three she had built with the house—Tommie awakened the security system's display panel.

"Don't talk to loud. I've secured the house, but we don't know if Lucien has the house bugged or has some sort of surveillance." Tommie explained to the women what had been going on and how shortly after finding out Lucien was the Holy Roller Bandit, they discovered that her partner John and Jillian were helping him on his bloody rampage.

"How did you figure out Jillian was involved?" Maria asked.

"Well, initially, the bibles that we've found at each scene were order by a Paige Guillory. We had totally forgotten that Jillian's middle name is Paige. So, we missed the mark on that one. But Guillory kept standing out until I checked with the Colorado Department of Corrections. That's how I found out Lucien had been released."

Maria and Kim were speechless. "But I no understand why Jillian would do this. She's our friend," Kim said.

"We don't know why she would do this either. I can only say that Lucien has done a number on her. Her self-esteem is so low, had it not been Lucien, it could have very well been someone else. I think she clung to Lucien because she was so familiar with him," Tiffany said.

"I found out that she's been connected to Lucien since the day he was convicted. She's visited him on a regular basis while he served time, put money on this books and one of the former guards admitted that he accepting money to turn his head during frequent conjugal visits. So they've been planning this for a long time. I just don't know how John got involved," Tommie said.

"What happened to John? Was he arrested?" Kim asked.

"No. John doesn't know we're on to him. My captain doesn't want to make any moves until Lucien has been apprehended. That's our main focus. John and Jillian are only a small part of this investigation," Tommie answered. She continued to monitor the security panels and motioned for the ladies to one monitor in particular.

"Take a look at this." She rewound the recorded feed and the ladies gasped when they saw Lucien rummaging through Tiffany's fridge. "This was earlier today when we were at the zoo. Look at the time stamp."

"He was here," Maria said, more so a comment than a question.

Tommie nodded. "He was here this morning. He left shortly after six." She rewound the feed a few frames and the ladies nearly choked when they saw Lucien leaving Jillian's room and disappear into the basement.

"The feed stops at the top of the basement stairs then we don't see Lucien any more. It looks like the monitor in the basement is out."

"Is he in the house now?" Kim asked.

"I don't think so," Tommie answered. "Everything was secure when I checked. If he is in the house, he's in the basement and he would have had to come in since we've been in here. But I can guarantee you that after our little phone conversation, he's out looking for Tiffany.

"I need to get out of here now," Maria said. All this was just too much for her. And she certainly didn't want to share space with a killer.

Tommie agreed. The ladies need to get somewhere safe. She knew her place was not an option so she decided that they would all check into a hotel.

Tommie gave the ladies instructions. "When we go back, I need you all to pretend as if everything is normal. I'm going to check the basement. I need you all to grab what's most important, but leave your luggage here."

The ladies all nodded in agreement. Tommie checked the monitors again, before Tiffany pressed the remote, opening the panic room. Once the ladies were out, Tiffany tucked the remote control back inside the hollow book and put it back in place.

The ladies acted if they hadn't a care in the world as they grabbed things like their electronics, clean underwear, a change of clothes and their purses.

Tommie drew her gun and ventured back into the basement. She needed to inspect why the camera by the basement door was not functioning. After she made sure no one was in the basement, she called Tiffany on her cell phone.

“Everything okay down there,” Tiffany answered.

“Yes, but I need you to check the alarm for me. I know we set it when we came in, but I just opened the door down here and the alarm didn’t go off. I think that Lucien may have cut the wires,” Tommie said. Tiffany checked the alarm panel as her friend instructed.

“It’s armed,” Tiffany said.

“Okay, let me check a few things and I’ll be right up,” she said before ending the call. Tommie checked the wiring and confirmed what she has suspected. The wires had been cut, which allowed Lucien to get in and out of the house undetected. Even though the door was locked, it was nothing for a professional criminal to gain access to a key. One thing Tommie was sure of, Lucien no longer had access to the attic. Tommie had made sure she double bolted the door and padlocked it. Not even Tiffany had a key to that padlock.

“What’s the verdict Detective,” Tiffany asked.

“He cut the wires to the security system as I suspected,” Tommie whispered.

The ladies grabbed what they had planned to carry and exited the house into the garage.

“Tiffany, I need you to leave your vehicle here. We’re going to rent a car and then take my SUV back to the station. If Lucien comes looking for us, it won’t be so easy for him to spot us.

“Can we talk now?” Kim asked, nearly bursting at the seams.

“This is crazy. Like something out of an NCIS or Law & Order show,” Maria said.

“Unfortunately, this is real,” Tiffany confirmed.

Twenty-Seven

Saturday, September 1, 2012

The Embassy Suites offered the ladies a good night sleep. With all that was going on, they needed it. As they showered and dressed, they planned out their day and decided they would have brunch at the Green Valley Grill and then head out to Sorella Day Spa for some much needed R&R.

"I may have to skip the spa. I need to go into the precinct," Tommie announced. "I'm waiting to hear back from Captain Randall on how we need to proceed with this case. I also need to check up on Jillian."

A waiter stopped by their table and asked the ladies what they wanted to drink. Everyone but Tommie settled on Mimosas, while Tommie settled for orange juice.

"I'm going to step outside and call the hospital. I'll be right back," Tommie informed her friends. When Tommie called the hospital to get an update on Jillian, the doctor told her that Jillian and the baby were doing much better. They were originally concerned about spotting, but found that it was due to stress. The doctor did warn that Jillian would have to take it easy or she would be in danger of losing her child.

Tommie was really at a loss for words. Her former friend—a woman she nearly knew all her life—was facing the birth of a child . . . and imprisonment. She was worried about the uncertain future of Jillian's unborn child. She didn't want the child growing up without his or her parents, but she knew Jillian would be in prison for a long time, and she was positive she'd keep her promise to Lucien . . . by the time his child was born, he would be dead.

The doctor gave Tommie more instructions and advised that if the test results she'd ordered came back normal, Jillian could be released later that evening.

Tommie thanked the doctor and asked for a security update from one of the officers. She learned that all was well, however, someone fitting Lucien's description had paid Jillian a visit.

"The subject checked in at the desk, said he was the victims brother and was looking for his sister. He gave a phony name. No information was given, however, before we could question him, he left the hospital. We've distributed his photo to the hospital staff. If he comes back, we will get him," the officer informed Tommie.

Tommie returned to brunch with her friends.

"Is everything okay?" Tiffany asked.

"Yes. As I suspected, Lucien tried to make contact with Jillian. He didn't get past the security guards though," Tommie said.

"I'm sure that ticked him off. No telling what he's going to do now. This could set him off for another kill," Tiffany said.

"I agree. He's gunning for us, especially me, so I'm sure he intends on heading back to your house if he isn't already there," Tommie told Tiffany. "With that being said ladies, we're going to have to cut this girl's weekend short. I could not forgive myself knowing that something happened to you. I'll pay for last minute airfare," she offered.

"No way. I hate to leave you guys here," Kim said.

"Me too," Maria said. "We don't want anything happening to you ladies either."

"I know, the less people we have to keep an eye, the better chance we have to catch Lucien and the faster the better."

"We understand," Kim said.

After switching the rental car with Tommie's police issued SUV, the ladies drove back to Tiffany's house to gather the rest of their belongings before heading back to the airport and their destinations.

"Tiffany, I really wished you'd either go stay with Kim or Maria for a while until this is all over."

"Absolutely not. I have too much to do, and you forget the conference is coming up."

"I know and Maria and Kim have to come back for it, so you can just come back with one of them," Tommie pleaded.

"Tommie, you're my best friend. I thought you knew me better than that. Because if you did, you'd know I'm not going anywhere. My life doesn't stop just because this jerk wants to go around terrorizing folks. He doesn't scare me," Tiffany said getting louder by the moment.

"Sorry I brought it up Jayne Wayne."

"Well I know one thing's for certain, Tiffany can't stay in her house. For all we know Lucien's there waiting for us now," Maria said.

"You could be right," Tommie agreed. "I want you ladies to get all your stuff. I'll check the house before we go in. Tiffany I want you grab some of your things—and Tiffany, you're not going on a forty day and forty night vacation. Just grab what you need okay?" Tiffany rolled her eyes at her friend.

"I'm serious," Tommie said. "I want to be in and out of here in less than thirty. Tiffany, you're going back to the hotel, but I'm going to tell John that we are taking you to one of our safe houses. That will keep him and Lucien busy for a while. So, make sure you grab your laptop and any of your important files. I need you to call your assistant and tell her not to come into the office for a few days. God forbid Lucien comes to your office looking for you and your assistant is caught in the crossfire."

When the ladies drove into the garage, Tommie got out of the SUV and drew her gun as she headed to the door.

"You guys stay here for a minute," Tiffany told Kim and Maria. She had gotten out of the SUV and opened the door to her Range Rover where she retrieved her Smith & Wesson .9mm. She entered her home after Tommie. The two inspected every inch of the house before allowing Maria and Kim in to get their things.

While they were upstairs packing the rest of their belongings. Tommie broke a key into the exterior lock on the back door. If Lucien got into the house, it wouldn't be through the door. They didn't have enough time to call ADT to come out and fix the locks. She needed to get the ladies to safety and catch Lucien once and for all.

*****

After saying a group prayer, Tommie and Tiffany gave both Kim and Maria hugs before each of the ladies boarded their prospective flights headed back home. They agreed to keep the girls updated on the status of the case and on Jillian and the baby.

Twenty-Eight

As Tommie exited the elevator and got closer to Jillian's hospital room, she could hear a commotion. It was Jillian demanding to know why she needed security outside her door and why the doctor hadn't yet responded to her request for a meeting.

"Jillian, Jillian! What's going on here?" Tommie asked trying to get a handle on the situation.

"Why the hell are there security guards outside my door and why can't I get straight answers from the doctor?" Jillian yelled.

"Calm down," Tommie said.

"I'm not going to calm down. I demand to know what the hell is going on here."

"Do you want to lose your baby? Because if you keep acting crazy, that's exactly what's going to happen. You're supposed to be on bed rest and relaxing."

"Don't try to handle me Tommie. Why are these guards outside my door?"

"For your own safety," Tommie would only say.

The doctor finally entered the room. "I can assure you that incidents such as this will cause you to miscarry. You cannot do this."

"Listen to the doctor Jillian," Tommie said.

"When can I leave? I want to get out of here now," Jillian demanded.

"As I told you yesterday, you have to find a way to keep calm. Are you *trying* to lose your child?"

"I want out of here now and you cannot stop me," Jillian yelled.

"Please understand that I advise against you leaving until your blood pressure is stable."

"I know my rights, you can't keep me here," she told the doctor.

"But I can. If you don't sit down and shut up, I'm going to have you handcuffed to that hospital bed!" Tommie told her. "Now, these doctors are trying to save your life and your unborn child's life. You're going to do what the doctor tells you and you will not give her a hard time."

Tommie and the doctor left the room as Jillian got back in the bed as instructed. She wasn't happy about it, but she didn't want to lose her child. She hadn't told Lucien she was pregnant yet. She motioned for the security guard to come inside her room.

"Excuse me, have I had any visitors," she asked in a more civilized tone.

"Only your friends," the guard responded.

"Are you expecting anyone?"the guard asked her.

Jillian thought against asking any more questions. As far as she knew, they still didn't know of her involvement with Lucien and she wanted to keep it that way. Lucien didn't know where she was anyway.

"No, I was just curious," she answered the security guard. "Do you know where my purse is?" The guard told her he'd ask the doctors or the detective where her belongings were.

The doctor returned to her room and informed her that her belongings were in the small storage closet in her room next to the bathroom. "I really don't want you getting out of bed, unless you absolutely have to. Would you like me to get something for you?"

"Yes, I need my purse."

The doctor opened the closet door and found Jillian's purse hanging one of the top hooks. She handed Jillian her purse and informed her that she would soon be sending a nurse in to retake her blood pressure.

"We really need to get that under control," the doctor said before leaving the room.

Once in the hallway, the doctor told Tommie, "You've got yourself a doozy in there Detective. I sure hope this over soon, because its disrupting my hospital."

"From your lips to God's ears doctor," Tommie responded. "It's my hope to have this guy caught very soon. We need Jillian to stay as long as you can allow her, because we are sure, she is on his list of fatalities."

"Let's play it by ear. Just make sure you keep me up to date."

"Will do," Tommie responded before leaving the hospital and heading back to the station. She received the call she was waiting for from Captain Randall.

Tommie arrived at the station shortly after leaving the hospital. As she always did, she dropped her bag on her desk and headed back to the Captains office.

"Detective," the Captain Acknowledged her.

"Captain," she responded.

"Catch me up to speed," he instructed her. Tommie told the captain about how she came to find that Jillian was in fact Paige Guillory and how strange her friend had been acting during their girl's weekend. She gave instances of Lucien's entry into Tiffany's home and other developing details.

"Tommie, you're too close to this case. First Lucien and now Jillian and John. I really have the mind to take you off this case."

"Please don't do that Captain. We're so close to catching Lucien. If you take me off now, the body count could rise and he could slip right through our fingers."

"If I leave you on, we could lose you, and that's not a chance I'm willing to take," the Captain said.

"But sir . . ." Tommie began

"I'm going to call someone else . . ." the Captain interrupted her.

"Please Captain. Give me until Wednesday. If I don't have him by Wednesday, then I'll remove *myself* from the case. I owe it to a lot of people to catch him sir. You have to understand that."

The Captain said back in his chair for a moment and studied his detective. He knew Tommie loved her job—and he knew she was good at it—but never had he seen her so determined to catch the bad guy. He was skeptical about keeping her on this case. He didn't want her emotions over clouding her ability to serve her duties as a police officer . . . her duty to serve the people. He thought what he'd do if this man had killed *his* mother, and was out to kill he and his friends.

"Alright Tommy, you've got until Wednesday night to catch this asshole. If you have *not*," he said emphasizing his point, "I *will* pull you off this case and send you on a long vacation until we *do* find him."

"Thank you Captain," Tommie said with relief. "I won't let you down sir."

"You never do Tommie. You never do."

The two put their heads together in an effort to come up with a strategy to catch Lucien Guillory and bring him to justice once and for all. The Captain informed Tommie that they couldn't keep Jillian much longer. They would have to release her or charge her with accessory to murder. It wasn't something they wanted to do right now, because it would blow their case.

"We're going to need to involve Detective Sykes in some way or another, otherwise, he too, will blow our case. I just cannot believe that one of our own would do something like this," Captain Randall said.

"You and me both. And I worked closely with him. Shared a few intimate details. Goes to show that you never really know a person. I mean, I've know Jillian since we were little. As you can see, my circle of friends is very small, and never in a million years would I have thought one of my closest and oldest friends would do something like this."

"That's why we must be alert at all times. Aware of everything and *everyone* around us."

Tommie nodded.

"Okay now, what are we going to do keep your friends safe during the remainder of this investigation?"

"I've sent Kim and Maria back home. They flew out earlier this afternoon. I tried to get Tiffany to go, but in her true stubborn fashion, she refused."

"That doesn't surprise me. However, since she is here, we need to assign her protection."

"I had her leave the house. Right now she's staying at a hotel. I have advised her not to go back to her office until this is over. I've also advised her to give her assistant time off. We don't need her getting caught in the crossfire. Oh, if you don't mind, I'd like John to believe that we've sent Tiffany to one of our safe houses. I believe this is going to help us and John will lead us right to Lucien," Tommie suggested.

The Captain agreed. "Okay, what's on your agenda for the next seventy-two hours?" the Captain asked her.

"Well, I've sort of rigged Tiffany's house. As you know, Lucien cut the wires to the alarm leading into her basement. I rigged the door so he couldn't get in. If he does manage to get into the house, he will have to break a window or set off the alarm to other parts of the house. Even if he gets in, no one will be there. He'll eventually realize that and try another plan."

The Captain listened attentively.

Tommie continued, " I think we should go ahead and release Jillian before Lucien gets wind and skips town. My guess is he doesn't know she is carrying his child. She will have to explain why she was in the hospital. I think between Jillian and John, we can flush Lucien out and cause him to make a costly mistake."

"I just hope it doesn't cost another innocent life," the Captain said.

"Me either. We have security detail on most of the women who were at the conference and I will be at my church finalizing plans for my first lady's celebration. As a matter of fact, I will be there Monday evening completing a few tasks."

"Okay. For tonight, I wouldn't advise you going back to the hospital to visit Jillian. I'd also advise you to be careful when going back home. I'm still confused as to why Lucien targeted 27 Flagship Cove and not your home."

"That is a little puzzling, but my guess is that either he wanted to torture me or the fact that my place is like Fort Knox. It's going to take a lot to get into it, and even a harder time getting out . . . *alive*."

Tommie was no fool and she learned from the best. Her father had taught her to keep herself protected at all times and to never let her guard down. He explained that this was especially important because she was female, she was single and she lived alone. Tommie had the top of the line security system, owned several firearms and had several other security measures in place—some of which no one knew about. She seldom had company at her home. Besides her girlfriends, she could probably count on one hand how many people she had invited to her home. Even John, her partner had not been invited, although she had been to his home on several occasions.

"Okay. Let's get some sleep and get this show on the road. We'll bring John in on a bogus plan and see where it leads us. But Tommie?"

"Yes sir?"

"You have until Wednesday to get this guy or you'd better pack for vacation."

"Yes sir," was all Tommie said before leaving to go home.

Twenty-Nine

Sunday, September 2, 2012

Dr. Rasmussen had had enough of her visitor's antics. Jillian had worn out her welcome with the fine folks at Moses Cone Hospital. The doctor had dozens of other patients to tend to—ones who wanted to be there and ones who wanted to be tended to.

"Detective Lane," the doctor said into the telephone. "This is Dr. Rasmussen. I'm calling you to let you know that we are releasing Ms. Dawson. I've run out of patience. I want to help you with your case, I really do. However, she is disrupting the care of my other patients, and I can no longer allow that."

Tommie had the mind to march directly to the hospital and arrest Jillian. She had enough evidence to arrest her on, but she knew doing so at the current time would jeopardize her case against Lucien and any chance she had in finding him. She knew that by letting Jillian go, her former friend would lead her straight to the Holy Roller Bandit.

"I understand Doctor. Thank you so much for being patient with us and for all your help." She ended her call with the doctor and called the head of the security detail that was assigned to guard Jillian. She instructed them that she wanted them to put a tail on Jillian. She knew Jillian would be calling Lucien to pick her up and Tommie wanted to know every move they made. The first day Jillian was admitted to the hospital, Tommie managed to insert a chip into her phone. She would be able to hear every phone call she made on the cellular phone.

Monday, September 3, 2012

Tommie was sitting at her desk when her partner walked into the precinct on Monday morning. She saw him before he saw her and pretended to be writing notes on a notebook.

"TL, how's it going partner?" the detective said.

"Hey John," Tommie said looking up from her tablet. "No real changes. Still trying to catch this creep."

"How was your weekend?" the detective inquired.

"You know I always have a great time when the girls are in town."

"I heard about your friend Jillian," Detective Sykes said.

Tommie tried not to act surprised, but she nor the Captain had said anything about Jillian. He had to have gotten his information from Lucien or Jillian. He was really getting sloppy. Tommie played the role to see how much John knew.

"She should be alright, just a little heat exhaustion. I think she's been working hard at work and it's just now catching up with her."

"Heat exhaustion, eh?"

"Yep," Tommie said. "How was your weekend?"

"Ah, nothing exciting, just a little yard work, some time with the Mrs." Detective Sykes said.

Tommie broke out in laughter.

"What's so funny?" Detective asked.

"It's just that I cannot for the life of me picture you doing yard work," Tommie said.

"What's that supposed to mean? I mean, before I put on the pounds, I did yard work all the time."

"It has nothing to do with your weight silly. It's just that you're always complaining that your gardener does a horrible job. I think you've complained about his work since I've known you and you've refused to get rid of him."

Detective Sykes gave a nervous laugh. "Well, I just wanted to do something different."

"What am I going to do with you?" Tommie ask laughing hard as she tried to keep herself from putting her hands around her partners neck and choking the life out of him.

Thirty

Lucien had to make his move fast. Tommie was getting too close to the truth. For all he knew, she was already onto him. His cohorts, Jillian and John had made too many mistakes—so had he. It all had to end now, but he wanted to make sure she knew why it was that she and the others had to pay. He wanted to torture her and share with her all the hell he had gone through while serving his fifteen years in that hell hole. It was because of her, those jurors, that judge and that prosecution that he had been judged and sent away.

After he finally made contact with Paige, he knew had to lay low, but that wouldn't stop him from carrying out his plans. It was such a shame, Paige had been so good to him, he had grown so fond of her, but now more than ever, he knew had to eliminate her. He had given her several chances to tell him about the child she was carrying, but she hadn't. That was fine with him. He knew a woman *and* a child would only slow him down. He knew after this was all over, he could not stay in the States. He would take his small fortune and move to an exotic island. He'd surely stand out with a woman and a child—something he couldn't afford.

* ****

"She's at the church," Detective Sykes said after he dialed Lucien's number.

"Are you sure?" Lucien asked.

"Yes, I just talked to her on her cell," John assured him.

Detective Sykes continued giving Lucien the low down on the church's schedule. He knew Tommie was working on a special project at Destiny Christian for First Lady Stowe's birthday . He also knew that most of the staff would be gone by six o'clock.

Lucien put his plan into action. He would have John arrive at the church around six-thirty, while he watched from across the street. He disregarded John's suggestion that he stay away from the crime scene, but Lucien thought John to be somewhat incompetent, he wanted to make sure the detective was worth the thousands he was paying him.

At six-thirty, Detective Sykes arrived like clockwork. He flashed his headlights to let Lucien know he was in position. He sat in the Ford Escort that Lucien had rented so that he would not be detected. Even if there was a make on the vehicle, it could not be linked back to John or to Lucien. One of the things about having Paige in his life was she was a valuable resource and knew her way around false identities. Neither Lucien or John knew that Tommie, Tiffany and the Captain knew who Paige really was.

Detective Sykes waited a few more moments before he exited the vehicle. He wanted to make sure Tommie was the only soul in the church. He sat and watched . . . and waited, as he thumped his fingertips against the steering wheel.

A while later, an attractive lady had exited the church. She looked professional in her tailored navy suit with a cream colored blouse. She had on low heeled pumps and carried a large gold purse. John guessed she was probably in her late twenties. He also guessed that she was probably the church secretary. He had seen her a few times before when he was casing the area. The woman got into her silver Honda Accord and drove away.

John surveyed the area once more. The only car left in the church parking lot was Tommie's unmarked SUV. John waited a few moments before exiting the car. He approached the church and looked around. The night air was still and carried a slight chill. The sound of the street traffic drowned out most sounds.

John checked the front door to the church, it was open. How careless, he thought to himself. Don't these people know that you can't go leaving doors unlocked? Even a church.

He took one last look around before he entered the church. Straight ahead was what he assumed was the front reception area. Directly behind it was the door to the sanctuary. A big marquee on the wall behind the desk read:

WELCOME TO DESTINY CHRISTIAN CHAPEL CHURCH, GOD IS IN THE HOUSE.

Right below it, was a sign that pointed to the church's business office.

Quietly, John followed the sign. Most of the offices were dark so he was sure the one with the light on at the end of the hall was where Tommie was. He quietly made his way down the hall, stopping short of the door. He could hear paper rustling. Not wanting to be detected, he stood still for a moment. Tommy was looking at files in a filing cabinet.

Tommie turned and headed towards the door. John managed to hide around the corner before Tommie was able to spot him. She headed towards the basement stairs. He waited until he was sure she had made it down the stairs before following her.

After Tommie disappeared into the basement, John counted to ten. "Ten . . . nine . . . eight . . . seven . . . six . . . five . . . four . . . three . . . two . . . one."

He took a deep breath and headed towards the stair well. He stood at the top for a moment to make sure Tommie was not coming back up. When he was sure, he tip toed down the old stairs and when he reached the multi-paneled light switch on the wall, he cut off the lights.

"What the . . ." Tommie begin to ask, catching herself, remembering that she was in the house of the Lord. She had been in this basement many times before so she traced her footsteps back to the light switch, only the intruder, whom she had not seen come in, hit her over the head with a blunt object, nearly rendering her unconscious.

Tommie fought with the pudgy intruder, each time trying to reach for her gun, until she felt a sharp pain in her shoulder, then her chest, then her thigh. She tried to scurry away and loosen herself from the madman, but he was administering jabs to her body any way he could get them and each time, the sharp object landed somewhere on her body.

The madman brutally beat the detective and administered his last blow with the knife to her face. He stopped, he had heard someone else there with him. He froze, as Tommie's faint whimpering faded into the darkness.

Detective Sykes wasn't taking any chances. Good thing for him he wore all black, leather gloves and a mask. He escaped up the stairs, out into the parking lot and fled in the Ford Escort.

Everything was dark, and through her blurred vision, Tommie couldn't make out anything. She was discombobulated and had no idea where she was or why she was in so much pain. She thought perhaps she had slipped in a puddle of water because she felt wetness all around her.

Trying to hone in on her senses, all she could make out was a faint pine smell and she could hear occasional traffic outside the structure she was in.

She tried to sit up as sharp pains filtered through her body, specifically her chest, arm, thigh and shoulder. She gasped when she felt the deep gash on her face.

"Oh my God, what's going on?" she shrieked. She followed the directions of the sharp pains and discovered there were deep, wet gashes everywhere she touched. Panic ensued her as she screamed for help. No one answered—just her echo shouting back at her. She tried to stand but her body thought otherwise. Instead, she crawled the area surrounding her in an attempt to find out where she was.

It was still pitch dark and no matter how much she tried to adjust her eyes, she could not see. She crawled a few feet ahead and ran into an object that came crashing down on top of her. She concluded it was a set of drums.

She was still for a moment and tried to think. She took in the smell of her dark, dank and musty surroundings.

If her memory served her correctly, the church stored an old drum set in the basement. This had to be where she was, because the floor was cement and it was cold. She pictured the room in her head. The light switch was forward about twenty steps and about fifteen steps to the left.

With all her might, she attempted to stand once more. This time, through all the pain she made it to the six-panel light switch and turned on the lights. She was right. She was in the basement of Destiny Christian. She had been in this basement several times before and knew old instruments and other church supplies were stored here.

She shrieked at the trail of blood that went from where she stood now to the huge puddle where she laid just moments before. With light now leading her path, she had a better view of her wounds. She assessed and counted—twelve from what she could see. She had been stabbed at least twelve times. And, with the pain that was spewing from her back, she was sure the count was higher.

Blood in several of her wounds had clotted, but the ones in her thigh and her left shoulder were still bleeding at a heavy pace. She tried feeling around her clothing for her cell phone, but couldn't locate it. She stood up to see if she could make it upstairs and to the offices of the church. Then—nothingness. Everything went dark again, and Tommie lost consciousness.

Thirty-One

The homeless man had slept here many nights. He knew the church's routine. He knew they had Sunday night services, Wednesday night bible study and special events on Friday. On those three nights, the church was usually closed by eleven-o'clock. On any other night, the church was shut down by six-o'clock after the office manager had left. He made sure the window he used to enter the church basement was unlocked, yet undetected.

He had sought shelter here from the elements every night for the last three years. During the day, he panhandled along busy streets and highways. He managed to hide his sleeping bag and pillow among old items in the church's storage room. Visits to the room were few and far in between. Even if the church was to stumble upon the mangy bedding, he could always obtain a new one from a local shelter or mission. The homeless man felt sleeping in the church was safer than sleeping in a multi-bed shelter. His arrangements worked for him and he saw no need to change them—at least not yet.

He had heard the commotion earlier. Detective Lane was on the women's board and the committee of women were secretly planning a celebration for First Lady Stowe. The homeless man had entered the church through the front door and assessed the sanctuary and business offices. The only two people in the church were Detective Lane and the church secretary. The homeless man made his way to the basement—to his nightly headquarters as he heard the church secretary.

"Sister Tommie, I'm headed out. Can you lock up for me?"

"Will do. Have a great evening," Tommie answered.

"I'll see you tomorrow." With that, the secretary exited the side door closest to the pastor's office.

The homeless man made his way to his spot. He had feasted on the McDonald's dollar meal and treated himself to a double cheeseburger, regular fry, regular Coke and two apple pies. He didn't want to run the risk of the aroma of food filtering through the church, so he never brought food in. Just bottles of water.

On this day, he was pleased. His twelve hours of panhandling had yielded him approximately four-hundred dollars and some change. He had resorted to panhandling when he returned home from Afghanistan. He was medically discharged from the United States Air Force after being struck by an improvised explosive device. And suddenly, the country he had fought for had forgotten about him. His medical benefits were minimal and he couldn't find a job. He had come home find that his wife of twelve years had taken his two small children and ran off with the man she was having an affair with.

He had lost everything and now, he had nowhere to go. The shelter would only let him stay days at a time and eventually his voucher ran out. And without a permanent residence so did his military benefits.

He longed to have a home of his own, but for now, he was content with his living arrangements. He had a nice warm place to stay at night—rent free. And if he was careful, he could shower and groom without being detected. He worked ten to twelve hours a day—tax free. He was able to eat a decent meal and catch an occasional movie. Never did he have to worry about Uncle Sam knocking at his door for yearly income taxes. But his mission was not for naught. He had a plan—he would save for another year or so, and then buy a condo. By then he hoped he'd have full time employment to maintain expenses, but if not, he could continue panhandling.

After hiding his day's earnings with his other savings in a pouch in his back pack, the homeless man settled in for the evening. His hard work during the day had allotted him the luxury of a Cricket pre-paid cell phone. This allowed him to watch limited television and radio programming so he was able to keep up with what was going on in the world.

So that he was not detected, he always used ear phones, keeping one bud in his ear and one out so that he could hear his surroundings.

He was watching a CNN report about the first African American and his re-election plans. Analysts had picked President Barack Obama and challenger Mitt Romney as front runners in the 2012 race. As far as he was concerned, neither of the candidates offered anything that would help him. He thought they were both a joke.

Suddenly, he heard something. It was the sound of footsteps and they were coming towards the room where he was.

The homeless man powered off his phone and stayed still. Then as soon as the footsteps stopped, he heard a loud crash. The footsteps then ran in the opposite direction. Shortly afterwards, the homeless man could hear Detective Lane entering the basement.

"Who's there? Are you okay?" No answer.

The homeless man could see the light come on under the door. He froze.

"Hello?" Tommie continued. "Who's there? I'm a cop and if you don't belong here, I suggest you come out now."

Tommie headed to a room in the basement that housed the choir robes. She turned on the light and looked around. Nothing. Just as she turned around, she spotted something unusual on the floor by the sink. It shouldn't have been unusual—after all, she was in a church. A bible was commonplace. But this one was different. As Tommie inched closer to inspect the bible, fear shot through her chest. She kneeled down to take a closer look.

The homeless man felt helpless. He saw it all from this vantage point—from the crack in the door where he had slept nearly every night for the last three years. He saw the unidentified gentleman crouched behind a row of book shelves. He was a black man and from what the homeless man could see, the man had an odd bump on his forehead.

Tommie opened the bible and dropped the bible when she read the inscription inside. *'He without sin. ~~Judge'* It was the inscription the Holy Roller Bandit left at every one of his crime scenes. Tommie immediately placed her hand inside her jacket and on her holster. Even though she was off duty, she kept her gun with her, especially when she was at the church.

Before the homeless man could give her any type of warning, the crouching man had come down on Tommie's backside with one of the old drums before escaping up the basement stairs. Even though she did not see his face, her attacker's stature seemed somewhat familiar to her.

The homeless man had seen the crouching man flee through the basement door. Before the door closed completely, the homeless man could see yet another man, a short, stocky man with a mask, come down the stair well, into the basement and shut the door behind him. The chubby white man only had on one glove as he entered the basement and quickly tried to put on the other as Tommie lunged towards him.

"Put your hands up!" Tommie yelled. Just as she spoke, the man had struck Tommie with a ten-inch blade—first in the shoulder, then in the abdomen. Tommie struggled with her attacker, and even though she got in a few good shots, her small frame was no match for the knife yielding man who invaded every inch of her with dynamic force.

The homeless man watched in horror as the angered man continuously stabbed at Tommie's lifeless body. Then, as quickly as he started, the man stopped, looked around the room and then stood up. The homeless man dare not move. If the intruder knew he was there, he'd definitely kill him too. He didn't dare try to close the door to his quarters—the killer would certainly come for him. He watched the killer as he apprehended the detective's gun, her wallet and her cell phone. With that, the killer turned off the basement light and fled up the stairs and into the darkness.

The homeless man looked out into the open room with fear. He wanted to go out and check on the detective, but his vantage point had been disabled. It was dark and he had no idea if the killer was still in the vicinity. He had waited for what seemed like hours before he decided he had to go for help. Just as he was about to step out into the darkness, he heard movement. As quiet as he could, he moved back and hid under his sleeping bag. He was sure the killer had returned to make sure he had finished his mission.

The homeless man shook in fear as he wondered how long he would have to stay and bear witness to the horrific scene. He also wondered if he would eventually be able to escape the church before anyone came in and detected him.

When the light came on, he nearly shrieked. He watched the detective as she looked around. And, a short moment after she was able to turn on the light switch, she had collapsed. He had been sure that the intruder had killed her, but he could see that the detective was strong and full of fight. He could no longer stand by and do nothing. He had to help this woman.

He had seen death in Afghanistan, and he, too, had a couple of kills under his belt. He also knew about survival instincts and this detective had them. He had served his country, defended it from the enemy. He had to help the helpless citizen.

The homeless man hid his fear, exited his living quarters, and headed for the detective. He had to be careful as there was blood everywhere. It was almost impossible not to get any on his shoes, but he knew the detective didn't have much time. He had to get her help. It was the right thing to do.

He kneeled over the woman and placed his index and middle fingers to her neck. He needed to see if she had a pulse. It was faint, but she was alive—barely.

The homeless man retrieved a few choir robes and dropped them in a heap at the detectives feet. He used his utility knife and began tearing the robes into shreds, using the shards to tie off blood flow to the wounds that were still oozing blood. Once he was able to contain the loss of blood, he sat the detective up and leaned her against the wall.

"Officer! Officer! I need you to wake up!" He softly patted her face as the detective's head bobbled from one side to the other. Then he heard the steps. He heard them run up the stairs, across the floor and then he heard the door being pushed open. Seconds later, he heard a car door close, an engine start and a car speed away.

"Ma'am. I need you to wake up!" the homeless man said. When Tommie did not respond, the homeless man took out his cell phone and dialed 911.

"Officer down! Officer down! 2200 Cone Blvd! Destiny Chapel! Officer down!" The homeless man didn't end the call, but laid his phone down to continue assisting the detective.

"Stay with me. Help is on the way. Lord Jesus, please intervene!" he shouted to God. "Please save her!" The homeless man ran to the sink in search of a cup so that he could fill it with water. He couldn't find any in the nearby cabinets so he returned to his sleeping quarters and retrieved a bottle of water from his hidden stash.

When he returned to Tommie, he trickled of water onto her face, then held her head back and into his chest. He poured a small stream of the bottled water down the detectives throat. She started coughing.

"Oh thank God, you're alive!" He held onto Tommie until she regained most of her faculties before it hit him—what if the police thought he was the one that had done this? He couldn't go to jail. When Tommy opened her eyes, the homeless man leaned her back against the wall.

"Glory to God you're alive. I did not do this. I did see who did, but I can't stay. I'm not supposed to be here and I'll surely go to jail," he told her before trying to make his exit.

"Please don't go!" Tommie pleaded with him.

"I can't be here when help arrives. They'll think I did this."

"I know you didn't," Tommie said, still groggy.

"Ma'am, you don't understand, I've been sleeping down here illegally. They'll surely arrest me and then try to accuse me of this. I must go now." The homeless man went back to his sleeping quarters to retrieve his backpack.

"Please! He may come back," Tommie pleaded. "I know you did not do this. I know you've been sleeping here for years now. I know you're a vet. I know you're homeless. Please help me. I will tell them you did not do this."

The homeless man shut his eyes and prayed to God for the answer. He did not want to go to jail, but he didn't want his conscious haunting him. He had helped many during the war. This woman here—she was one of them—an American, a protector of the law. He had to help her. It was the right thing to do. It is what God would want him to do.

"His will be done," the homeless man said to no one in particular. "His will be done."

"How do you know who I am?" he finally asked Tommie.

"I remember talking to you a year or so ago. You were panhandling on Wendover and I-40 one day and you nearly got hit by that eighteen wheeler. Do you remember . . ." Tommie rubbed her head. The homeless man held a stitch of cloth to the wound on it.

Tommie continued. "Do you remember? We went to the Sheetz on the corner, and I bought you a cup of coffee. You told me about how you served in Afghanistan only to come home to find your family gone and no help from the government."

The homeless man thought back. This woman had remembered him from over a year ago and he couldn't say the same. How could anyone forget someone like her? Even in her current state, he could tell she was a beautiful woman.

"Wait a minute," he said, as if a light bulb had gone off in his head. "Your dad passed away. He was a cop too, right?"

"That's me?" Tommie smiled.

"I'm so sorry this happened to you detective."

"Call me Tommie," she said. "If it hadn't been for you I probably would have died."

"I wish I could have done more. I wish I could have stopped that guy. I was a coward. I've killed people in war, and I couldn't stop that lunatic from attacking you."

"I'm just glad you're here now. In all your years sleeping down here, I bet you never thought you'd see anything like this."

"You knew?"

"Of course. I'm detective Tommie Lane. I know *everything*." Tommie shut her eyes. He could tell she was trying to ignore her pain. "I watched you on a regular basis. You know, for your safety and for the safety of the church."

"And you didn't arrest me?"

"No. As long as you didn't cross any boundaries. I knew your story. Besides, you were in by midnight and out by five a.m. No harm, no foul."

Sirens could be heard from the basement and the homeless man felt relieved that Tommie would get the medical attention she desperately needed. "Your father would be proud," he told her. She gave him a weak smile. He could tell she was about to fall back into unconsciousness.

Thirty-two

"Greensboro Fire Department!" they both heard from upstairs.

"We're down here!" the homeless man screamed. "Down in the basement. Please hurry, she needs help!" he was doing everything he could to slow down the blood that was escaping his new found friend. He held the torn cloth on various wounds on her body. Tommie did her best to help, but she was growing weaker by the moment.

"Is there anyone I can call for you?" the man asked Tommie.

"Yes, please call my friend Tiffany," Tommie said. She gave the man her friend's number. When the homeless man got Tiffany's answering machine, he held the phone to Tommie's ear.

"Leave her a message," he said.

"Hey Tiff, it's Tommie. There's been an incident. I think they are taking me to Wesley Long. Please call me back at this number I am calling from or meet me at the hospital." She motioned for the man to end the call and he did.

Several firemen stampeded down the stairs and into the basement coming to Tommie's aid. "What happened?" one of them asked, not specifically to the detective or the homeless man. But, by the looks on their accusing faces, they were coming to their own conclusions.

"I was attacked," Tommie said weakly. "And if this nice man hadn't come along, they would have killed me." Their expressions changed. One of the firemen asked the homeless man a few questions about what he had saw. The man answered the questions and diverted his attention back toward Tommie.

"She's a police officer. Detective Tommie Lane," the homeless man said proudly. "She's one of Greensboro's finest."

Paramedics, followed by several uniformed officers, entered the basement. The paramedics ran to Tommie's aid while the officers made sure the area was secure.

"Is there anything broken?" One of the paramedics asked Tommie as he cleaned her wounds. Another applied pressure on her oozing wounds with gauze, while yet another went over her medical history, asked if she had any allergies and was she up to date on her immunizations.

After cleaning her wounds with topical meds, the first responders advised Tommie that she should go to the hospital to get checked out. Tommie couldn't remember the last she had a tetanus shot, so it was suggested she get one just in case. After a bit of hesitation, she agreed. She wasn't sure what she had been stabbed with, and the last thing she wanted to do was get an infection.

Out of the corner of her eye, she could see her partner appear in the doorway. *How convenient*, she thought. For all she knew, he could have been the one that had attacked her. As a matter of fact, she was willing to bet her money on it. She searched around for her cell phone so she could call her Captain to let him know what had just happened and that she thought John was behind it.

She motioned for the homeless man to come to her. When he got close to her ear, she whispered, "Can I see your cell phone?" The homeless man nodded and Tommie motioned him to give it to her. Instead of calling her Captain, she decided to text him.

John just tried 2 kill me. I'm at DCCC headed 2 hospital. Danger.

She whispered in the homeless man's ear once more, "I promise to return your phone when I'm done. Are you okay with that?" The homeless man nodded.

"Tommie! What the hell happened?" asked Detective John Sykes making his way to Tommie and the homeless man. John looked at the homeless man oddly and wondered who he was.

"He was here," Tommie said.

"Who?"

"HRB," Tommie answered. She paid close attention to the expression on John's face. He tried to act surprised but really wasn't. Tommie couldn't let on that she knew he was connected to the Holy Roller Bandit and she knew he was the one that had attacked her. She had to play her cards right. If there was one thing her father taught her, it was that sometimes the answer was right under your nose and that even those closest to you could betray you—at the right price.

"If it hadn't been for this gentleman, he would have killed me." John eyed the homeless man.

"What's your name sir?" John asked him.

"Oh, I'm nobody. Just happened to be in the wrong place at the right time sir," the homeless man said.

Detective Sykes grabbed the homeless man's arm, "I asked you a question. What . . . is . . . your . . . name?"

"John, what are you doing?" Tommie asked coming to the homeless man's defense.

"How do we know this transient isn't the HRB?"

"I know for a fact that he's not," Tommie said. "Now let him go!"

"Not until he answers a few question," Detective Sykes said handcuffing the homeless man. Then turning to the paramedics he said, "We need to get her to the hospital STAT!" With that, the paramedics put Tommie on a gurney and carried her to a waiting ambulance.

The investigative crew started navigating the crime scene. Detective Sykes eyed the homeless man then joined the investigative crew, pretending to be looking for clues. He wanted to make sure that he had left nothing behind that would implement him. He noted the excessive amount of blood and located the exact point of struggle. He checked each of the storage closets, coming across the one the homeless man had been taking refuge.

With the exception of the sleeping bag, there was no evidence of the homeless man. He surveyed the area one last time. It was a good thing he wore gloves. He noticed a bloody finger print on the inside of the door leading out of the basement. He debated whether to clean it up or not. He looked around to see if anyone was looking. The homeless man was.

"How did you get in here," John asked the homeless man. Sensing something was not right, the homeless man exercised his right to be silent.

"I asked you a question!" the detective snapped. Still, the homeless man said nothing. John got closer to the homeless man's ear—out of ear shot of the others and said, "You know, I have ways of making you talk." He stuck his night stick in the homeless man's ribs. The pain caused him to fall to the floor, as Detective Sykes pulled the handcuffed man back to his feet.

"I'm going to ask you one more time. What's your name?" Again, the homeless man refused to answer. The detective struck him once more with his stick. Again, the man whimpered and fell to the floor.

"In Jesus name!" the homeless man finally shrieked.

"Oh, not even Jesus is going to save you," the detective smirked.

"Do you guys have this under control?" John asked the investigative team.

"Yes sir," one of them answered, showing concern for the homeless man.

"Good. I'm taking this one in. He may be our suspect, or know something about the attack on Detective Lane." The crew nodded and continued collecting evidence.

The detective practically dragged the injured man up the stair, as he taunted him.

"It really doesn't matter what you know or what you saw. You won't live long enough to tell anyone," the detective threatened. The homeless man knew there was a good chance that the detective would carry out his threat. If he could just get free of the handcuffs, he could make his escape.

He was more worried about Detective Lane. Her wounds were extensive and it appeared that she fell in and out of consciousness. One thing he knew for sure was Detective Lane didn't trust the night stick wielding man and his faith in God told him he'd be seeing Detective Lane again—but on better terms.

Thirty-three

Once he had secured the homeless man in the back of his patrol car, Detective Sykes drove to a secluded area. Once he was sure he was out of sight of prying eyes, he turned down an abandoned road and into a forested area.

Even though he was trembling on the inside, the homeless man showed no fear. He had faith and knew that God's will would be done. One thing he was sure of was that he had accepted Jesus Christ as his savior, and had repented and been forgiven of his sins. He was at peace.

The man looked around searching for an escape route. He looked around the patrol car for something that could help free him. That's when he saw the leather gloves and the droplets of blood on the floor of the patrol car. Suddenly things were becoming clearer to the homeless man. He had a hunch why Detective Lane distrusted this man.

"You've interfered in the wrong business," Detective Sykes told him. "This is how it's going to go down. You interfered in an ongoing investigation, you were arrested and then you tried to escape. There was a struggle in which you tried to take my firearm and the gun went off. You were just a useless casualty. "

The detective gave the homeless man a hideous smirk, but the man did not flinch. The coward before him did not scare him. He had fought to defend his country against outsiders—men far braver than he. Never had he imagined he'd have to come home and defend his country from insiders as well.

Detective Sykes turned his attention to his cell phone and dialed. "What the hell happened? She's supposed to be dead!" Lucien yelled into the phone without any formalities.

"You weren't supposed to go in. What in the hell did you do that for?"

"I had to leave my calling card," Lucien said smugly.

"You could have jeopardized the whole plan. And, she wasn't breathing when I left. I was sure she was dead. I stabbed her multiple times," the detective yelled back.

"Well she's not dead! And you were so messy you left a witness."

"I heard someone else come into the church, so I got out of there. Looks like he was already in the church. According to Tommie, he saw the whole thing. But don't worry, I have him now."

"Then you know what to do with our little friend don't you?" Lucien asked.

"Yes," Detective Sykes said and ended the call. He sat there or a few moments thinking to himself. When Paige had initially approached him about the proposition her friend Lucien had, he thought it would be easy. He'd just get rid of Tommie and he'd get paid fifty-thousand dollars. He was so close to the case, it should have been a cinch. But it wasn't, a homeless man had stuck his nose where he shouldn't have.

Detective Syke's thoughts were interrupted by his car radio. "Charlie-Adam-three-six-nine, we have a report that suspect Holy Roller Bandit is in a standoff with officers. Reported hostages."

Puzzled, the detective forgot about the threats he'd made to his backseat guest, and headed to the location of the standoff. When he pulled up, there were over a dozen Greensboro police cruisers at the scene. They had the home in question surrounded.

Detective Sykes exited his patrol car and approached an officer that looked as if he was in charge.

"What's the deal?" he asked.

"We've got the Holy Roller Bandit inside. We know he's got at least three hostages."

"Are you sure?" John asked perplexed. Was there a copycat on the loose? He had just talked to Lucien in his patrol car. "How do we know it's him?" he asked his fellow officer.

"He called the precinct and said he had hostages and wanted to exchange for Tommie." Detective Sykes was sure this was either a copycat or Lucien was setting him up.

"I think he's a copy cat," he said turning to the commander.

"What makes you say that?" the commander asked.

"Because the HRB just attacked Tommie at Destiny Christian Chapel."

The commander looked confused and watched Detective Sykes walk back to his police car. Once inside, John called Lucien on his cell phone. Once Lucien answered John said, "Something's going on. I think you should leave town, but not before paying me my money."

"What are you talking about?" Lucien asked. "

"Someone pretending to be the Holy Roller Bandit, called into the precinct saying he has hostages and he wants Tommie in exchange. I'm on scene now and they have this house surrounded. Where are you?"

"27 Flagship Cove. I have Tiffany. Were you able to take care of our little . . . problem?"

"No, right after I hung up with you, I got the call over the scanner about this hostage situation. But don't you worry, I'll take care of . . ." Detective Sykes gasped when he looked into the back of his patrol car to find the homeless man nowhere in sight. He looked up and down the street to see if he could see where he could have gone. He did not see the homeless man but what he did see caused him to drop his cell phone on the floor.

"Step out of the car with your hands up, now!" Detective Sykes looked around to see who the officers were talking to. It became evident as the officers closed in on his car.

"Get out of the car now!" one of the officers said as he opened the detective's car with his gun cocked.

"What's going on here?" he asked confused.

"Up against the car detective!" the officer commanded.

"C'mon, what the hell's going on here?"

"Detective Sykes, you're under arrest for attempted murder and conspiracy to commit murder. The officer read the detective his rights.

"I don't understand," the detective resisted. He was sure Lucien had set him up.

"Sir, please. Let's not do this the hard way," one of the arresting officers told him. John looked around in confusion as a black police issued Crown Victoria with tinted windows pulled up. It parked in front of his patrol car and John was surprised to see Tommie get out of the car.

"Aren't you supposed to be in the hospital? Who let you out? You're in no condition to be here," he told her. He was right, Tommie was in pretty bad shape, but there was no way she was going to let Detective Sykes, the Holy Roller Bandit and Jillian get away with murder.

Tommie approached him and stood only inches from his personal space. "We've been partners for how long John?"

"Five or six years, why do you ask me that?" Detective Sykes asked in confusion. "Tommie why are you here? You should be recovering."

"Five or six years. And, over those five or six years, I've shared my entire life with you—my strengths, my weaknesses. And I just couldn't believe that someone I called friend and trusted with my life would betray me, let alone try to kill me. And for what? $50,000?"

"That bastard!" John yelled.

"Where is he?" Tommie demanded.

"What? Who are you talking about? What's going on here?" John had a million questions.

"Never mind, I have an idea where he is. Read him his rights and book him," Tommie demanded the arresting officer. "And make sure we do everything by the book. We don't want this slime bucket slipping through any loopholes."

"But Tommie . . ." The detective pleaded.

"I'll make sure your wife and children know exactly what kind of scum you are. I hope it was worth it, because it will be a cold day in hell before you see them again."

Detective Sykes grew angry as he struggled with the officers and tried to grab one of their guns. He wanted Tommie dead just as much as Lucien did at that very moment.

Before the detective could gain control of the loose gun that hit the ground, Tommie let off a round in the detective's leg.

"You shot me!" he yelled.

"You're lucky that's all I did. You're not getting off that easy. They just love your kind in the slammer," she said. "Now get him out of here!"

Thirty-four

Tommie made sure the parameters of Tiffany's house were covered before going in. When she got the okay, she used her spare key to enter the house. She had to be careful. She knew her had returned home, her life could be in danger.

"Hey Tiff, it's me. You home?" she asked when she entered the home at 27 Flagship Cove. "Tiff, it's Tommie." She didn't have her gun drawn, but she made sure it was ready and tucked away in her back holster.

"Tommie!" Jillian said when she saw Tommie. She leaned in for a hug but Tommie backed away from her.

"Jillian, what are you doing here?" Tommie asked. "I thought you were back in Denver. When did you get in?" Tommie tried to appease Jillian to get as much information from her former friend to make sure she, Lucien and John stayed locked away for a long time. Tommie knew this had to end and it had to end today.

"What's wrong?" Jillian asked Tommie.

"Where is he?" Tommie asked.

"Who?"

"Don't play dumb with me Jillian. I know everything. And where is Tiffany? You better not have touched a hair on her body or I'll shoot you myself."

Jillian's whole demeanor changed. "He made me do it," she told Tommie. "He said if I didn't he'd kill me."

"Cut the crap Jillian. I know that you've been involved with Lucien since before he went to prison. He was like a step father to you. He was my mother's boyfriend and you go and do something like this? You disgust me!"

"You've always thought you were high and mighty. All of you. Always looking your nose down to me . . ."

"No one looked down at you. You did that all by yourself. You're mad at the world because you had to take care of your father. How selfish of you. That man gave everything he had to make sure you had what you needed. Lucien killed my mother in cold blood, you're supposed to be one of my best friends and you help this low-life try to kill me and my friends? I do hope you know that once he was done with you, you'd be added to his list of casualties. He's only been using you to fund his mission."

"You see, that's where you're wrong. Lucien loves me. I'm the only woman that understands him. He'd never do anything to hurt me. Besides, I hold the key to all Lucien's money—money he didn't even know he had."

"Are you that dumb? What happened? You're so beautiful, so educated and so talented. Was your self-hatred so bad that you'd let this fool brainwash you?"

"You're jealous aren't you Tommie? A woman working on the police force, no family, no man. The fact that Lucien chose me and not you makes you green with envy doesn't it?"

"You are sick and you deserve whatever you get. Where is Tiffany?" Tommie asked drawing her gun.

"She's right here," Lucien said finally abandoning his cowardly shadow. He had Tiffany close to his body and a gun to her head. She tried to speak but Lucien had her mouth taped with duct tape. She was bound by a rope at her wrists and ankles. In addition, Lucien had a noose around her neck. Judging by the bruises on her face and her torn clothing, Tiffany put up a fight.

"Let her go!" Tommie demanded.

"I don't think you realize who's in charge here," Lucien said. "This is going to go how I say it's going to go." Tiffany struggled to break free of Lucien's hold, but he hit her across the back of the head with the butt of the gun he was holding to her head.

"You're not going to make it out of her alive you bastard," Tommie told him. She looked at Lucien for a moment. She had always wondered what her mother had seen in him. Even though they were divorced, her father tried to talk her mother out of getting involved with a man who was suspected of killing someone. She wondered what it was about this man that made women act stupid and fall under his spell. She wanted to ask him after all this time why he killed her mother, but she didn't have time to play catch up. At this point it didn't matter.

"That's where you're wrong. Not only am I going to make it out of here alive, but I am going to kill you and your friends before I do."

Jillian looked at Lucien in horror. "You mean her friend right? Singular."

"Well Paige . . . Jillian . . . Which is it?" Lucien asked her.

"Both. It's Jillian Paige."

"Looks like you've been holding out on me my darling. I'm wondering what else I don't know about you. I'll tell you what I do know—I know about the money you stole from me. Not that it will matter, but never keep private information in the same place you lay. If you do, make sure it's secure."

Tommie watched the banter between the two and realized how it was that Lucien was able to get Jillian to do whatever it was he wanted her to do. She had no self-respect for herself and around Lucien, she appeared child-like.

"I've stood by you all this time and you question my loyalty?" Jillian asked Lucien. "I've given you money, helped you kill the others and did anything you asked me to, and you question me?"

Jillian stood directly in front Lucien. "How dare you question my loyalty. I wasted fifteen years of my life while you were in that hell hole, putting money on your books, taking care of things for you on the outside, having sex with you in that disgusting prison, on unclean bunkers and mattresses while the guards stood nearby. I stood look out when you killed those jurors, those police officers, those ministers and other ladies from those churches. And that attorney, I was the one that trapped him for you." Jillian was finally getting a set of brass ones, but it was too late, much too late.

Tommie paid close attention, looking for her chance to get a clear shot at taking Lucien out without hurting her friend. At this point, she was no longer concerned about Jillian.

"Have I told you that you talk too much?" Lucien asked before raising his hand, pulling the trigger and shooting Jillian in the middle of her forehead.

As soon as she dropped to the floor, Tommie took her chance. She shot Lucien center mass, just centimeters away from Tiffany's head. Lucien dropped to the ground and Tiffany fell with him. Tommie ran to her friend's aid, but she had to make sure Lucien was dead first. She checked his pulse. It was confirmed, Lucien's crime spree had come to a deadly end.

Several officer rushed in to take control of the situation. Another officer double checked Lucien for a pulse to make sure he was dead while Tommie checked on Tiffany. She had fainted when Lucien was hit. With a couple whiffs of smelling salts, Tiffany came to and screamed when she saw Lucien's dead body lying next to her.

"It's okay. He's dead." Tommie held her friend, who cried in her arms like a baby. Tommie could only imagine the horror that Tiffany had gone through. They both looked over at Jillian's dead body.

"I can't believe she would do this," Tiffany said.

"That's because we were all too busy with our lives, and I was so enthralled in this case. Even you gave her the benefit of the doubt. To me, there has always been something off about her. I mean way back in high school."

The paramedics made their way to Tiffany and checked her out. "I think she will be okay, but we need to take her to the hospital for observation," one of them said. Tiffany tried to protest but Tommie wasn't going to let her win.

"I'll be there as soon as I'm done here," she told her. Tiffany wasn't going to argue with her friend. After all she had been through, she had no fight left in her.

Thirty-Five

Wednesday, September 4, 2012

Tommie found Tiffany's hospital bed empty when she peeked into her room at Wesley Long.

"I believe she is in the restroom," one of the nurses said as if she was reading Tommie's mind. Tommie smiled and entered the room.

"Is that my best friend with my favorite coffee?" Tiffany called from the bathroom.

"Yes ma'am," Tommie answered.

"I'll be out in a minute."

When Tiffany emerged from the bathroom, she was fully dressed.

"Looks like you're ready to go," Tommie teased.

"You know I do not like hospitals." Tiffany leaned in and gave Tommie a hug. "I didn't get a chance to thank you for saving my life. So thank you and thank you for the coffee. How did you know?"

"Are you hungry?"

"You know I am," Tiffany laughed. "They had nerve to bring me some brown stuff they tried to pass off as meatloaf. I told them I wasn't eating that crap." Both the ladies laughed.

"Are you okay?" Tiffany asked Tommie. "How did things go down after I left? What about John?"

"I'll tell you all about it over vittles."

"Vittles? Oh my goodness! You've been in North Carolina *too* long!"

"I know right? Where would you like to have brunch?"

"Hmmm. There's this new place in downtown Greensboro called Tavos. I hear they have this awesome buttermilk chicken corn muffins to die for."

"I've been there, and they do have great food. But I hate to disappoint you, those muffins are nothing more than the Jiffy corn muffins you used to make, but with a little kick."

"Sounds good to me," Tiffany shrugged.

After the two ladies were seated at Tavos, and had placed their orders, Tiffany asked the waiter, "Can we get a few of those great muffins I keep hearing about?"

The waiter smiled, "Coming right up."

"So, Detective Lane, start from the beginning," Tiffany said once the waiter was gone.

"Well, I'll give you the condensed version," Tommie said.

"No, I want to hear every last detail," Tiffany said. "We've got all day."

"Well, you see. It started back in 1973 when my mother met Lucien," Tommie started.

"Don't be a smarty pants. You know what I mean," Tiffany said, rolling her eyes at Tommie. Both the ladies laughed.

"Like I said, the condensed version. I'll give a more detailed version when we conference call with the other ladies tonight."

Tiffany nodded her head in agreement as she took a drink of lemonade. "Can you believe that after *all* this time Jillian has had it out for us?"

"I never could have imagined she had it out for us, but I told you that girl wasn't right back when we had our very first girl's weekend. At first I thought she was just stressed out because she had to take care of her sick father," Tommy said.

"Yeah, I thought the same, but she got stranger each time we saw her. I started believe it was more than that, but I could have never imagined."

"You're telling me. But, it looks like she was brainwashed by Lucien," Tommy added.

"Well there's more to it than that. It just so happens that Jillian, oops, I mean Paige and Lucien hooked up right after her father died. She wasn't innocent in that transaction."

Tiffany looked at Tommie in disbelief. "But Lucien was like a second dad to us. That girl could have had any man she wanted."

"I agree. I just don't see the attraction there," Tommie said looking off into space.

"Well, wait a minute now. Lucien was a good looking man back then," Tiffany smirked.

"Yes, but he was old enough to be her father."

"True," Tiffany agreed.

"Anyway," Tommie continued, "I believe Mom found out about Lucien and Jillian and that's why he killed her. If you know anything about my mother, you know she confronted him—and probably with hot grease."

"Yes that sounds like your mother," Tiffany laughed. "Loved her to death but she was crazy." They both laughed.

"Now that I think back to the trial, Jillian was even a little different then. She didn't want to pick a side. She stayed neutral and I caught her on several occasions communicating with Lucien in the courtroom—whether it was eye contact or a head nod."

"Hmm," Tiffany said. "It's funny how you see all the signs but never connect the dots until after the fact."

"True. During all this, I couldn't figure out why Lucien left that inscription in those bibles. But after calling my buddy in Atlanta . . ."

"Is that man still after you?" Tiffany interrupted her friend.

"Yes, Mike is still trying to flirt. But it's harmless."

"Yes, Mike. That was his name. Umhmm. Mike and Tommie," Tiffany teased.

"Shut up!" Tommie laughed. "Anyway! Mike pulled Lucien's other records for me and he had done the same thing back in the seventies. You remember—when he was accused of killing that other woman."

"Yes, the one he was accused of killing and was on trial with when he started dating your mother. I've always wondered what she was thinking when she met that man and when she decided to stay with him, even after the fact. Then she drove around in that car with him—the one they found the blood in and was said to have killed that other woman in."

"I can say that I never understood my mother, and that is much of the reason we were so much different."

"Not *too* much different," Tiffany intervened. "Both of you are crazy—or were."

"Hush. Lucien's jacket showed the same m.o. for that murder as well. His attorney at the time said Lucien vowed to get revenge on everyone who tried to lock him up. He killed at least three people, but it all stopped after he and my mother visited his parents in Atlanta. And, none of the evidence could place Lucien at any of the crime scenes."

"That was when your mother got sick and your family believed his mother put a root on her right?"

"Yes," Tommie answered.

"Tommie, have you ever thought that maybe your mother knew about those murders in some way or perhaps she was the reason he stopped?"

"Truthfully Tiffany, after I read that jacket, part of me felt that my mom may have even been some sort of accomplice. Maybe that's why he killed her. Maybe she got tired of him beating on her and she told him she was going to go to the police. Honestly, I don't know."

The waiter placed a basket of warm cornbread muffins and butter on their table as well as the drinks they had ordered.

"So Jillian was working with Lucien to kill all those people?"

"Yes. And those people were only casualties. Lucien was really after me. He vowed to get everyone involved, including my friends and then, I was to be his last victim."

"So Tiffany had to know that Lucien was going to get her too," Tiffany said.

"She suspected it, but wasn't sure. But I talked to Lucien's family. His mother had left Lucien a large amount of money before she had died. It seems that Jillian intercepted the account information and hid the money."

"And Lucien had no idea?"

"No. The entire family disowned him when he was sentenced to prison. Well, everyone except for his mother. It wasn't until after their mother died a couple of years ago that they followed their mother's final wishes and sent a letter to Jillian, which she was supposed to deliver to Lucien—but she never did."

"So I'm a bit confused, how did your partner John get involved with this?"

"Can you believe that a-hole? All those years and he turned on me."

"I can't believe that either. What did the GSO end up doing with John?"

"He's in jail. But he's facing so many charges, I hope they fry him."

"Did he ever say why he did it?" Tiffany inquired.

"What else? Money."

By the time Tommie had gotten into the meat of the story, the waiter had returned with their entrees.

"These muffins are to die for," Tiffany said. "Can we have a few more?" Tiffany asked the waiter.

"Certainly. I'll be right back with those," he said.

"For a moment I was wondering if you were talking about him or the cornbread, you were staring so hard."

"That little boy is gorgeous!"

Tommy rolled her eyes at her friend and continued her story.

"So, after I was attacked at the church . . ." Tommie started.

"How did Lucien get into the church?"

"John. And it was actually John who attacked me. Lucien just wanted to get in to leave his calling card."

"The bible?" Tiffany asked.

"Yes. But if it hadn't been for that homeless man, I wouldn't be here."

"Homeless guy?"

"Yes. Do you remember me telling you a while ago about a homeless man I met peddling on off Wendover and I-40?"

"Yes, the one that had come home from the war and ended up losing his family and everything else."

"Yes, that's the one."

"How is he involved?"

"Well I knew he was living in the basement of the church. He has been for the last two years."

"The last two years? How does a man go undetected in a church for two years?"

"I knew he was there. And, I figured as long as he didn't harm anyone, I wasn't going to bust him. He came in late at night and was gone by early morning. I made sure I kept my eye on him."

Tiffany looked at her friend with a strange look.

"He was harmless. The guy had lost everything. I wasn't going to deny him a warm place to lay his head. Especially since he didn't bother anyone. He brought in his own water—never food and he used his cell phone as entertainment. Besides, no one ever went into that basement. I had it under control."

"Go on," Tiffany said.

"He happened to be there early the night I was attacked. He saw everything. He was the one that called the police and kept me alert until they got there. I thought it was all too odd that John showed up right when the fire department did. It was as if he was right there waiting." Tommie explained to Tiffany all she knew about John's involvement and how Paige had approached him with Lucien's *"can't refuse"* offer.

"I had already told my captain and after I was attacked and taken to the hospital, we set up a trap for John. We knew he would lead us to Lucien. And just like clockwork, when we sent out a fake hit on the Holy Roller Bandit over the wire, we knew John would show up. We wanted him to think that Lucien had set him up. But he didn't expect to see me."

"I bet he nearly had a heart attack when he saw you," Tiffany said.

"He thought I was dead and kept asking me what I was doing there. After we apprehended him, we knew we would find Lucien."

"27 Flagship Cove," Tiffany said nodding her head. She could no longer call it home and would be calling her realtor as soon as she could to put it up for sale. "How did you even know I'd be there Tommie?" Tiffany inquired.

"Because I know you, and you're hard headed. I was so scared when I got to your house. I thought Lucien had killed you. I wanted to shoot Jillian as soon as I saw her but I wanted to assess the situation first."

"*You* were scared? When Lucien didn't shoot me, I was sure *you* were going to take me out when you shot him. I can't believe you shot me!" Tiffany said as if she had just had a great revelation.

"It was either shoot you and disarm Lucien or let him kill us both. You'll heal," Tommie said with a sudden sense of seriousness. "I could have lost my best friend in that house," Tommie said grabbing her friends hand and holding on for dear life.

"But you didn't. I'm still here."

"And for that I'm thankful."

"Poor Jillian," Tiffany said.

"I didn't feel sorry for her. Not after she put all our lives in danger."

"I'm also glad we got Kim and Jen out of there. We're going to have one hell of a girl's weekend next time."

"You're telling me. You know," Tommie sighed, "besides saving my best friend and finally putting an end to Lucien's crime spree and catching a bad cop, one good thing did come out of all of this."

"What's that?" Tiffany asked, stuffing her face with buttermilk fried chicken.

"That Jillian and Lucien didn't leave their offspring," Tommie said.

Tiffany nearly choked on the flavorful bird. "That's not right! That baby was innocent."

"That's true, but with those genes and being raised in the system, there's no telling how that child would have turned out. It couldn't have been good."

"You're right, I just hate that the baby had to pay for its mother and father's crimes," Tiffany frowned.

"Well I guess it's up to you to give us a baby," Tommie said.

Tiffany's yes got big. "Waiter!" she shouted to a nearby waiter. "I need a drink!"

Also by ***Yolanda M. Johnson***

Revelations
a novel
Yolanda M. Johnson

About the Author

YOLANDA M. JOHNSON-BRYANT, also known as "That Literary Lady", is the author of Circumstances, Revelations and other novels. She is currently working on her children's, teen and tween series, the That Literary Lady Knows series, and the second installment of the Tommy Lane Detective Series and a host of other projects.

When Yolanda isn't writing or spending time with her family, she enjoys being a career Toastmaster with Toastmasters International and a mentor and volunteer for Junior Achievement and the Women's Resource Center of Greensboro. She is a technology and social media geek and loves giving workshops on literacy, self-publishing and social media. She is the owner of Bryant Consulting and Literary Wonders Media Group. She is the founder of the non-profit Sweethearts of the Triad, an organization that recognizes and supports women entrepreneurs and community leaders of the Piedmont Triad area of Greensboro, North Carolina. She enjoys traveling and has three beautiful grandchildren. She and her poet husband, reside in the Piedmont Triad area of North Carolina. To find Yolanda on the web, just "google" her.

Her websites are:

www.yolandamjohnson.com

www.yolandamjohnsonbryant.com

www.lwmediagroup.com

www.sweetheartsofthetriad.com

www.thatliterarylady.com

www.literarywonders.com

www.bryantconsultingonline.com

Social Media Keywords:

Yolanda M Johnson-Bryant

That Literary Lady

www.ingramcontent.com/pod-product-compliance
Lightning Source LLC
LaVergne TN
LVHW050635100826
845148LV00011B/1872